# SARAH AND ME AND THE LADY FROM THE SEA

Sarah and I went into the kelp, brushing it apart with our free hands and kicking the slick strands away with our feet. They looked like big brown snakes. Ugh!

The first things we saw in the kelp were two feet, very white, bare ones. It was a *person* in there! Now we really tore at the kelp, getting it out of our way. We worked from the feet on up. First we saw some white cloth with a rope around it—the rope was tied around the person's legs. Then we got up to the waist and saw more white cloth and more rope, then to the shoulders, which also were tied up. Tied up? *Why?*

It was Sarah who uncovered the person's face. It was a young woman. She was beautiful, so beautiful, in fact, that she made me catch my breath and think of sleeping princesses and damsels in deep distress. Her braided hair was long and pale gold, and her eyebrows and lashes were dark. Her face looked like it had been carved out of snow, it was so white. Her eyes were closed very tight, and she moved her head from side to side, whimpering.

# BY PATRICIA BEATTY

# SARAH AND ME AND THE LADY FROM THE SEA

## PATRICIA BEATTY

A BEECH TREE PAPERBACK BOOK • NEW YORK

The Library of Congress has cataloged the Morrow Junior Books edition
of *Sarah and Me and the Lady from the Sea* as follows:
Beatty, Patricia
Sarah and me and the lady from the sea / Patricia Beatty.
p. cm.
Summary: When, in 1894, their father's business failure forces the family to
live in their beach home on the penninsula just above the Oregon border,
twelve-year-old Marcella and her younger brother and sister find the experience
much more rewarding than they imagined, especially when they become
friends with the numerous members of the Kimball family.

[1. Seashore—Fiction.   2. Self-reliance—Fiction.   3. Friendship—Fiction.
4. Washington (State)— Fiction.]
I. Title   PZ7.B380544Sar   1989   [Fic]—dc20   89-33624   CIP   AC

First Beech Tree Edition, 1994.
ISBN 0-688-13626-5

*To my brother, Tip,*
*Colonel Phillip W. Robbins, U.S. Army, Ret.*
*who is the other "captain's kid,"*
*and to his "lady," Doris*

# CONTENTS

# 1
## OUR SUMMER PLACE

That Monday morning, the big, dark-haired Kimball girl who worked for us during the summer brought us our mail from the Nahcotta post office as usual. After she had carried in the breakfast for the four of us Abbotts, she took an envelope out of her apron pocket and said, "There's a letter for you from Mr. Abbott again, Missus."

Mama said, "Oh, yes, his Monday letter. By the time we come up here to Ocean Park for the summer next year, the telephone lines should be installed. Then

Mr. Abbott will be able to call us and not have to write. Did you know we've had telephones down in Portland since 1892, Anna?"

"Uh-huh, Missus Abbott, you told me that before. All four of you have told me that. That's what's wrong with big families. Everybody's always repeatin' himself. You ought to hear what it's like when all eight of us kids are at home at the same time."

"Yes, I can just imagine." Mama, who wasn't interested in Anna's family, stared at the table and asked, "Anna, where are the strawberry preserves?"

"Right under your nose, Missus, in the little covered bowl." The hired girl gave a sniff and left for the kitchen.

Nobody who lived summers at the beach would ever say that the beach people who worked for us were like the servants Mama hired in Portland. The people there were quiet and soft-talking and polite. The beach people didn't much like summer people and they often let us know it.

The minute after Mama had had her first sip of coffee and set the cup down, she opened Papa's letter. She read his big handwriting fast. Suddenly she let out a soft little cry. "No, no, not yet! That's what I was afraid of." I saw her hand go to her heart. "Oh, dear, it's worse than I'd thought. Bankers do not have hearts."

I'm Marcella, the oldest of the three Abbott children. At twelve I'd learned that the world could sometimes be a place where wicked things happened to a person who didn't deserve them to happen—like having your pet bird get loose and get caught by a neighbor's cat or your horse breaking a leg and getting shot or getting the mumps the day before you were going on a school picnic. But bankers and hearts?

I asked, "What's wrong, Mama?"

She shook her head. "I'm afraid, children, we won't be returning to Portland next month, but will be staying on here in the house Grandmother Grover willed to us when she died. We've got to stay to help your father out in his troubles."

*"Stay all year long?"* asked Florence, my ten-year-old sister.

"Yes, that long for certain and more than likely even longer."

Alec, my nine-year-old brother, squeaked, "We'll be stuck here *all the rest* of 1895 then?"

Florence didn't give Mama time to reply to Alec. She said, "But we always leave the beach by the first of September!" Her greenish-gray eyes had got dark with worry, and she was twisting her blondish-brown hair around one finger as she did whenever she was upset. She looked like Alec and me, and we looked like Mama, who was from a very old Portland family, the Grovers.

Alec asked, "What about Papa? Where'll he be?"

"He'll have to stay in Portland, Alec. He has a lot of work to do," replied Mama.

*3*

Working? Papa working? That wasn't any real news to any of us. He'd sent us to the beach with Grandmother Grover and Mama every summer for as long as I could remember. We'd figured our summers would always be spent on the peninsula part of western Washington State for the rest of our lives. But to stay here all year long? The only time Papa ever spent with us on the beach was the one week in June when he'd take time off from our dry goods store and come up on the train to get us settled in for the summer. He'd hire a beach girl to do the work in our summer house and he'd vacation with us for a few days. Then back he went to Portland.

He'd gone home ten weeks ago to our big brick house on Park Street. I missed him and was looking forward to being with him the rest of the year. Papa usually kept his mind on our cloth business, but when he took all of us out to dinner in the nicest restaurants in Portland, he was fun to be with. We got to dress up then in our Sunday best, and I liked that.

I asked, "Why will we be staying here at Ocean Park all year long?"

Florence added, "It ain't natural, Mama."

"It *isn't* natural, Florence. Somehow you've been in the company of the local people so much that you're beginning to talk like them."

I put in, "Well, it really isn't natural." I hadn't given in to the Peninsula people's bad grammar.

"No, it certainly is not," she said with a deep sigh.

*4*

"Then how come it's happening?" asked Alec stubbornly.

"Children, I didn't want to tell you our troubles and upset your summer before now. It's all because of that terrible flood last year, when the Willamette River came all the way to the second story of the Abbott building on Front Street."

Alec said now, "The flood was fun. I liked going around town in a rowboat and not having to go to school. I went fishing and caught a carp out of the second-floor window of our store before it got flooded."

"Of course, being a boy, you would, Alec." Mama turned angry now, but not at him. "The plain fact is that the merchandise your father had ordered taken from the first floor and stored on the second for safety's sake got soaked through by the dirty floodwater, too. The cloth was worthless when it got dried out. It was shrunk all out of shape. Who would have thought the water would go that high?" Now she was melancholy again. Mama changed moods fast at times. She went on, "Your father had gone to the bank to borrow money to buy all that lovely British woolen cloth. He hadn't expected a flood, of course. Who did? Now the bank he borrowed from is calling in his loan and wants the money back. In order to pay the bank and keep our store, he has to sell our house in Portland and some other things as well."

"Sell our house?" cried Florence.

Mama nodded over the handkerchief she'd pressed to her face. "And the carriage and horses. It's all in the letter here."

"And Dandy, too?" cried Alec.

"Dandy, too."

I sat amazed. Dandy was the white pony the three of us owned. He'd been a Christmas present to us two years ago. I said, "It's sure a good thing Prince Albert's here with us. Does Papa say we have to sell him, too?"

"No, Marcella. The dog's too old to be of any value, even though he's a pedigreed English bulldog."

We were quiet for a while after that. Then I said, "Mama, does this mean we'll be going to school here on the Peninsula at Nahcotta?" I was smart enough to know she'd make us go to school even on the moon.

"Yes, Marcella. It is not a private school like St. Helen's Hall you and Florence attended in Portland. Your father will live with his sister and her husband while he tries to put his business affairs in order. Aunt Florence offered to take you, Alec, so you can go to school with your cousin Arthur."

We all turned toward Alec, who looked as though he'd had a hatpin, a long one, stuck into him, his eyes bulged so. He said, "I don't want to go live there even if it is Portland and Papa's living there, too! I don't want to have to live like Arthur. He has to keep on whistling every time he goes into the pantry so his papa knows he isn't eating anything in there. No wonder he's so skinny! No, I don't want to live with Aunt Florence and Uncle Mack."

"Neither would I," said Florence, who'd been named after Papa's oldest sister.

"I'll write your father that you will be staying here with us then, Alec. I agree with you about your Uncle Mack," said Mama, surprising me.

I asked, "What are we going to do, Mama?"

She sighed. "Not a blessed thing, it seems, but stay here. Your father is sending up our winter clothing, and he'll arrange that I have money every month for household expenses. He'll join us when he can, perhaps at Thanksgiving and Christmas."

Just as she said the word "Christmas," I heard the back door of the house bang, and I knew that meant either the big Kimball girl had gone out to feed Prince Albert in his doghouse or somebody had come to visit her. Peninsula people who worked for summer people were inclined to have lots of visitors coming through the back door.

Mama had set the letter down beside her plate with the words, "We have to be sensible about this, my dears. We can't add to your father's burdens by complaining and wailing. We shall try to make the best of it." A little crooked smile came over her face. "We'll try to think of this as an adventure. This house is big and old and drafty, but we can spend a winter here if we must. We own it, so we don't need to pay rent, thank goodness. We'll have to take in our belts a bit, however, and do our own housework."

"I don't know how," said Florence.

Mama said, "Then we'll just have to learn. It can't be very difficult. Look at all the people who do it all the time for years and years."

"Can you cook, Mama?" I asked her.

"Not really, except for molasses taffy and things like that. But there are cookbooks here in the house. I've seen them in the kitchen. They must have been used by your Grandmother Grover's cooks at one time. Now eat your breakfast. I'm going upstairs to lie down as soon as I've done. Now eat, please."

Nobody had much of an appetite after Papa's bad news, so we just picked at the eggs and ham and toast. When we were through, Mama rang the little silver bell beside her to let the Kimball girl know she could come get our dishes.

She sailed in right off, gave us all a strange look, grabbed and stacked our plates, and went back to the kitchen.

I followed her to see what I could see and, if I didn't see anything, to go out and untie our dog.

Yes, the Kimball girl had visitors, another black-haired girl, but younger by the look of her, and along with her a golden-haired smaller girl with big, deep-blue eyes. I'd seen these girls in the Nahcotta store earlier that summer. They looked the same today. Both were wearing faded calico dresses and were barefoot. We Abbotts never went barefoot anywhere. Mama wouldn't let us and I didn't really want to.

The Kimball girl started the kitchen pump going to rinse the fried egg off the dishes before boiling them in soapy water in a big pan on the stove. Meanwhile, the girl nearest my size stuck out her tanned hand, grabbed my pale one, and said, "I'm Sarah Kimball. I'm twelve. This is my little sister, Evangeline. She's almost nine." Because I was staring at Evangeline as I held Sarah's hand, Sarah explained as she let go, "All of the rest of us Kimballs take after our pa. He's dark. Evangeline takes after our ma."

Evangeline shook her butter-colored curls, nodded, and said, "We're sure sorry that you're gonna have to sell your house and pony down in Portland."

Sarah added, "Take heart. It ain't bad living here all year round. Us Kimballs have always done it. We like it. It can be interesting here at the beach. I'll be your friend if you want me to."

I couldn't answer her for a minute, I was so angry. They were surely nosey. Finally, I got out, "How did you know about our house and our pony?"

I saw how both Evangeline's and Sarah's eyes went to the back of their big sister, who was busy at the sink. Of course, she'd told them the minute they had come in, while we were finishing our breakfast. Anna Kimball had been listening behind the closed kitchen door. Mama had always suspected the beach people listened in on the summer people. Well, our sorrowful

*9*

news would be all over the Peninsula by tomorrow morning. They didn't seem to need telephone lines here.

I wanted to stamp my foot. It wouldn't be ladylike, but it would sure make me feel better. Instead I only gave the girls icy-cold looks and went out through the kitchen door, letting it bang behind me.

I knew there could be bad ocean storms in the winter here, and we might be cold and damp, but I figured we could get through those things. But what about dealing with the people here? Grandmother Grover, who had died four years ago, had always called them the "wild natives," and she'd been a very intelligent lady. We Portland Abbotts had always kept to ourselves when we summered at the seashore, or we associated only with other summer people we knew.

The two younger Kimballs followed me out of the house, banging the door, too. They came up to where Alec and Florence were getting Prince Albert ready to go for a stroll over the dunes to the ocean. They'd come out the front door, which had been smart of them.

An old, long and lanky, gray-muzzled red dog was beside Prince Albert's doghouse, sniffing it and then sniffing our dog.

Sarah Kimball told us, "That's Red, our dog. He knows your dog from our coming here before, visiting our sister. They ain't about to fight. I think maybe they're both too old for that anymore."

Alec said, "Once Albert gets his jaws on another dog, he never ever lets go."

Florence said, "That's right."

Well, that was nonsense. Our English bulldog hadn't ever been fast enough in his life to catch hold of another dog. All he was was a barker and growler, but with that big head of his and bigger jaw he had scared quite a few Portland dogs in his younger days, and he had enjoyed it.

I said, "Prince Albert has to go for a walk now. Please excuse us."

I reached into the box beside the doghouse that held our sun parasols and told Alec, "Today is your turn to hold your sunshade over Albert, and it's Florence's turn to share hers with you." Because Prince Albert is white, he sunburns—mostly on the nose. So we have to watch him all the time.

Now I heard the Kimballs start a tittering laugh. Then Evangeline said, "Your dog *sunburns?*"

"We all do," I told her. "That's why we wear long sleeves and long stockings."

Sarah said, "Being barefoot's fun. Are you sure you sunburn?"

"Maybe not, but we don't plan to find out. It's what Mama wants. Portland folks we know stay pale," Florence told her.

Off we Abbotts set at a slow walk with Prince Albert in tow. He had the big body and short, crooked legs of his breed of dog, so we had to take it slowly with him.

That red dog followed us, and so did the two Kimball girls.

Suddenly Evangeline cried out, "I got a good look at your kitchen. You haven't got a Nickel-Plated Beauty in it like we have in ours."

I turned around. "What in thunderation is that?"

"A stove. The finest iron cookstove on the whole Peninsula. We Kimball kids earned enough money to buy it for our ma one Christmas."

"Evangeline, you didn't earn a red cent!" her sister corrected her. "You just got born the night the Nickel-Plated Beauty was delivered for Christmas. I earned money, though. I picked berries." She turned to us to say, "You have to come see it. We keep it up just fine."

I told her, "Oh, for goodness' sake! Who wants to see an old stove? What's important about stoves?" I opened my parasol, and off we went with Alec leading Prince Albert while he sheltered him from the late summer sunshine. I figured if we ignored the natives, they would drop off before long. As for the one who worked for us, Mama had paid her only to the end of August, three days away.

After a long spell of silence except for the sand

squishing under our shoes, Florence said, "Marcella, do we *have* to go to school with them?"

I said, "Only five days a week, Florence." I said it lightly, but I'd been thinking the same thing. They belonged here on the Peninsula. We didn't. They were like the seagulls. We'd been birds of passage like wild geese were.

I looked behind me now and saw that those two pesky Kimballs had taken a plank road that led over the dunes to their right toward Ocean Park, where they lived along with us. Their red dog still trailed us, though. To get rid of him, I opened and shut my parasol a couple of times, making a whooshing noise, and he began to run in the opposite direction. I'd seen him at the ocean running free. He had a bad habit of biting the waves, and I didn't want Prince Albert to start copying that and sneeze, too, from the salt water.

Tears suddenly stung my eyes. I was surely going to miss all the nice things about Portland—the restaurants and theaters and rose gardens and parks. The seaside was fine for summers, but only for summers. I'd miss my girlfriends at St. Helen's Hall, and what about Dandy? Would our pony get a nice, kind owner who wouldn't ever use a whip on him? And, oh, how I'd miss Papa! I'd miss him so much it would hurt. But I knew we just had to stick it out here because that would help him in our money troubles.

As I walked along beside my brother and sister, I thought about Papa's letter and what it meant for us Abbotts. It could mean some hard times ahead with us fending for ourselves. With all our summer-people friends gone back home, we'd be stuck with the "natives" if we were to have anybody at all to talk to besides ourselves. But being here by ourselves wouldn't be too bad, maybe. We had games and books, and we were all good talkers. And we'd write letters to our friends in Portland as well as to Papa. I'd start writing tonight to Jessie and Jennie Palmer, the two sisters who were my best friends at school. They'd write me back, and I'd be glad to read their letters, even if what they had to tell me about their schooling and visiting and shopping would make me homesick.

# 2
# THE OLD DICKENS AND A NASTY SURPRISE

Just after Anna Kimball left, Mama and Florence and I went to the kitchen to look at the pots and pans in the cupboards. My goodness, but there were a terrible lot of them—big ones and little ones, round ones and square ones, heavy ones and light ones. Some had handles, some didn't. Some were blue-speckled, others were dull black or shiny black.

Mama said, "Oh, I should have spent more time in the kitchen at home when I was a girl. I do imagine that the pots with wooden handles go on top of the stove. Otherwise the wood would burn up in the oven."

I figured that had to be true. To comfort her I said, "I bet the cookbooks will tell us what kind of pot or pan to put things into."

"I surely hope so, Marcella, but that isn't what worries me most of all."

"What does?" asked Florence.

Mama pointed. "It's that stove over there, my dears. I've heard talk about kitchen stoves. Chan used to curse our Portland stove whenever he cooked on it. I didn't know what he said because it was in Chinese, although I could tell from his tone that he was cursing. I presume your father will let him go now."

Florence and I turned to look at the wood stove, too, and all at once I shivered. It was old and big and coal-black without any shiny copper or brass on it— not even a nameplate or any comforting curlicues. The way it squatted like a toad on its short, crooked legs made me feel it didn't like us. It was much bigger than the woodbox beside it, full of the wood that Anna had chopped that morning. Alec would be doing that chore from now on.

Mama said, "My lady friends in Portland have told me that their cooks complain about stoves being cantankerous. They claim they have personalities just like human beings do. They have to be lit in a special way to suit them, and then there's all that fuss about dampers and vents and other things. I wish now I'd just once lit a fire in a kitchen stove."

I told her, "I can light one in a regular little parlor stove. I did it once at school when the French teacher got sick and had to go home early. It wasn't so hard to do."

Mama shook her head. "But you didn't cook on that, Marcella. You didn't bake meat or bread."

"No." To make her feel better I added, "But we could heat up canned stuff on top of our parlor stove."

"So we could, but it's so small. Perhaps we can do that until I learn to cope with this stove. We've got quite a lot of canned food in the pantry and we could get more from the store when we need to." She nodded. "We'll all go there together very soon and lay in supplies. They can be delivered by wagon. Children, we will need more than food if we're to winter over here. You'll have to have raincoats and hats and boots to go to school. This is a most rainy place in winter, even rainier than Portland, I'm told, and it can be stormy, too. You'll have to walk to school, of course."

This made Florence and me sigh. Papa had usually driven us all to school in our carriage on his way to work, even on sunny days. We knew where the school was here in Ocean Park, but it was almost a mile away, and we would have to walk along the railroad tracks and over trestles with scummy green water under-neath. Just thinking about the trek was enough to make us weary.

The first morning without Anna Kimball doing our housework, we walked to the general store at Nah-cotta, a mile away. It was a strange place. It sold every-thing under the sun, from clam shovels and fishnets and crab rakes to calico and gingham cloth, life pre-servers, horse harnesses, teakettles, whiskey, candy, dog biscuits, deer rifles, and bonnets. Just about any-thing the beach people could need was on counters, in barrels, stacked against the walls, or hanging from the rafters.

The storekeeper, Mr. Willard, a tall, skinny, shiny-haired man, came to meet us after we'd tied Prince Albert to a porch post in the shade outside. "What can I do for ya, Missus Abbott? I hear you're staying on through the year 'cause you folks got business trou-bles down in Portland. I'm sorry to hear about that. I know what business troubles are, having gone flat-busted one time myself. I'll try to help you out any way there is and give you the lowest prices I can. You'll be needing help, I betcha."

I turned to watch Mama after he'd talked awhile. With every word he'd said she'd gotten taller and stiffer. Finally she told him, "Well, we shall do just fine here." Now she took the list from the beaded bag at her wrist and handed it to him. "This is what I think we shall require. Can you have the things on my list delivered today, please?"

He took the paper, put on spectacles, and read the list slowly. "Canned fruits and vegetables, canned beans and meat—lots of canned stuff. Rain gear for the kiddies. Kerosene for your lamps. Crackers and biscuits, coffee beans. That's all right, but bread ain't. Folks around here bake their own bread, Missus Abbott, and don't sell it."

Mama said sharply, "That's all right. Strike that off, then. We'll bake our own. What will I need for it?"

His glasses slipped down his nose. "Huh? Oh, flour and salt. You probably got them things, but you'll be wanting yeast."

"All right, then add yeast to the list."

"Ma'am, you don't have potatoes or onions on your list, and it's too late to grow them in gardens around here."

"Well, add those also."

"I will." He was grinning now. "Is that all you'll be needing?"

Mama's glance took in the pistol on a rack on the wall. She pointed. "Will I be needing that?"

He shook his head. "Nope. Us natives are law-abiding for the most part. It ain't like Portland up here. We ain't got no burglars around. Everybody knows how things have gone sour with you. You won't be pestered. One hard knock in life's enough."

I felt my face getting red with anger. Curse that

Anna Kimball and her sisters! They must have got on horseback to spread the bad news about us all over the Peninsula. They were real Pauline Reveres. How I hated them at that moment! I hated the storekeeper, too. He knew he was the only general-store keeper in Ocean Park and we'd have to buy from him whether we wanted to or not.

All the way home I knew we had bad thoughts in our heads about the tattletale Kimballs and that rude man, Mr. Willard, but being ladies and gentlemen, we didn't say them aloud. Even Prince Albert started growling because he caught our mood.

When the rickety old delivery wagon came late that afternoon, the skinny, black-haired boy who drove it carried our grocery boxes inside. He unloaded the boxes to take them back, but stayed behind awhile looking our kitchen over like he owned it.

Because Mama was lying down upstairs with a headache, I was the one who talked to him. I told him, "You don't have to stay to get paid. Mama paid at the store for all of this."

He said, "I know that. Mr. Willard told me. He said you was cash customers. I been living in Oysterville working for some folks there as a hired man when I ain't delivering for old man Willard. What I do is better than cutting wood for the railroad like Pa does. Hey, I know that old stove of yours. That's the Old Dickens! That's what my sister Anna called it, and so did my sister Clarrie, when she worked here for your Grandma Grover."

I asked, "Are *you* a Kimball, too?"

"Yep, I'm Tom. Anna said she sure had a tussle with that stove." He laughed. "Lots of girls who've worked here learned to cuss its insides. Anna won't be working for you next summer. She'll be going to high school in Ilwaco next year, but this year she's earning money by working for Ma's sister, Aunt Rose Perkins, who runs the Palace Hotel in Nahcotta. Anna lives there now, and says she likes what she's doing because she gets to meet lots of new folks at a hotel, not just one summer family at a time."

I held my temper in, though I felt insulted.

He went on. "We Kimballs all got good jobs except for Sarah and Evangeline, who're still in school." He started ticking off his family on his fingers. "Anna and Sarah and Evangeline, that makes three. Then there's Whitney, the oldest one of us, and Cameron. They're fishermen on Willapa Bay and got their own boat. That's five. Then there's me, that's six. Clarrie works over the Columbia River in Astoria training to be a nurse. Then there's my big sister, Hester, who's got the best job of all of us. She's a—"

I cut him off. I was so sick of Kimballs by this time that I didn't want to know what this Hester did. Who cared? I said, "Thanks for bringing us all this stuff."

As Tom stacked boxes to take them away to the

wagon, he told me, "I hear tell not one of you Port-landers has ever done a lick of work."

This made me flare. "Papa works very hard!"

"Sure, with a pencil. I mean real work that takes muscles. Us Kimballs are hard workers, all of us."

I flung after him, "And you're big talkers. You're braggers and worse—tattletales."

I heard his laugh from behind the boxes he lugged. "Beach people always talk about summer folks. We know you make fun of us and call us 'natives' like we were cannibals with bones in our noses. So we talk about you behind your backs. Turnabout's fair play, kiddo."

I yelled, "I hope my dog out there takes a chunk out of you!"

"He won't. He's lying outside his house sound asleep."

Saying this, Tom stacked the boxes in the wagon, got up onto the seat, clucked to the horse, and left. I watched him from the window, raging. Next time he came with groceries, I'd make it a point to let Mama deal with him.

Once I calmed down, though, I started getting depressed, remembering what Tom Kimball had called our cookstove and what Anna had told him. If she had struggled with it, how about us? I could see lots of canned-pork-and-beans suppers ahead for us, warmed up on the parlor stove. And that stove had taken me twenty minutes to light after we'd got home from the store.

I'd had to bend over and put in sticks of kindling, then paper, and then light the paper with a match. After that I had to wait beside the open door for a while, looking into the belly of the stove and getting my face singed while the kindling caught fire. After it caught, I could lay in small sticks of stovewood, and when they caught fire I could put in bigger sticks. It all took time and I risked burning my fingers as I poked around inside getting things burning strong enough to keep going by themselves.

And Mama had said we were to see this as an adventure. Some adventure!

It wasn't only the cooking and housecleaning that were problems, but the washing and ironing, too. Mama had never lifted an iron in her life. In Portland we'd sent Papa's and Alec's shirts and our sheets to a Chinese laundry. Mama's and Florence's and my clothes had gone to a French laundry where ladies ironed ruffles and laces perfectly. Now that was something more we'd have to learn to do.

Today at the store Mama had bought six big bars of ugly yellow soap to use in the huge oval copper pan I'd seen Anna Kimball boil clothes in. But Anna had done that on the Old Dickens! Our whole lives were coming down to that wicked-looking stove. We just had to tame it. Mama would have to learn how and learn it quickly. She'd be the only one at home on school days to feed it—and feed us on it.

We had a bean-and-crackers supper heated on the

parlor stove that night, and for dessert, canned peaches and pears and chocolate-covered biscuits from a tin. Everything was all right except that we had to drink water. There was no fresh milk, and though we had coffee beans, we didn't know how to fix them. Florence tried to make us tea, but the leaves got stuck in our teeth because she put in so many of them.

As we rinsed off our dishes under the kitchen pump, Mama told us, "We must arrange to have milk delivered, or get a cow. But I do not plan to deal with a cow right now."

Alec said, "Marcella and Florence can walk to Nahcotta tomorrow and look for cows in pastures along the way and find out who owns them and ask the people to bring us milk. Or we can carry it home with us on the way back from school if we find a farm close enough."

I asked him, "Well, Mr. Alec, what will *you* be doing while Florence and I hunt for cows?"

He looked sternly at me. "I plan to start figuring out the kitchen stove. I'm the man of the house here."

Florence giggled and told him, "Uh-huh, brave men always duel with dragons in books I've read."

He glowered at her. "That old Anna Kimball got it working all right. If she could do it, I can, too. We have to roast those coffee beans we got at the store and grind them before Mama can make coffee. I already learned that from one of our cookbooks. I can read, too, you know."

I looked to Mama, who said, "That's right, we do. I know living here all year will not be easy for a time, until we get the hang of things, but I do not intend to exist without my morning coffee. It isn't civilized."

Florence added, "And I want my hot cocoa and chocolate eclairs and vanilla ice cream." Suddenly she began to cry, digging at her eyes with her fists as she ran out of the room.

Though I wanted to cry, too, I didn't. I asked, "Mama, while we hunt up cows for milk, do you want us to look for butter and cream, too? Cows and butter go together."

"I know that, Marcella. Please do. We just have to keep our heads in this emergency." With a dripping plate in her hand, she went on. "I think I have been a useless woman for too much of my life. I should have been shown how to fend for myself better, but I was never taught—not even given the chance. When I wanted to do anything but sew a fine seam or play the organ, your grandfather used to tell me, 'Now don't you bother your pretty little head about that. That's men's business.' Your father was the same. Your grandparents picked him out for me, and I must say I truly love him, but he should have kept me better informed about our affairs." She sighed. "I guess it comes from always having been rich. I feel quite worthless here, my dears—no help to you at all. You girls must not grow up useless, too. I want you to learn what the world is about and in time even to vote.

Someday women will be permitted that privilege and duty."

I ran to her, grabbed her around the waist, and said, "You aren't useless at all. You make Papa and Florence and Alec and me happy, and you made Grandma and Grandpa happy, too. People who make others happy aren't ever useless. Isn't that so, Alec?" I glared at him to get the right reply.

He came up with it. "Sure, Marcella." He sounded absentminded, though, and I could see his mind was on other things. He was scouting out the stove, lifting its lids and moving its grates and dampers and frowning as he did. Just like a man!

The next day Florence and I found a meadow full of black-and-white cows. Keeping clear of them because they were so big, we followed their tracks back to a barn and farmhouse. A woman was by the chicken coop scattering corn for the hens. She listened to what I said, nodded, and told me, "My boy'll fetch you milk every other day and home-churned butter once a week on his way to work in Ilwaco. How're you doing for eggs? I can sell them, too, but not my prize laying hens. Will you need eggs?"

"Oh, yes," I told her.

"How many will you be wanting?"

Florence looked at me. "How many, Marcella?"

"I don't know." I blushed.

The woman laughed. "Eggs generally sell by the

dozen. You'd be the summer Abbotts, wouldn't you? There's four of you, I hear, so two dozen a week ought to do it. The Kimball girl who worked for you used to bring them every week from her house. You got milk and butter from there, too. Didn't you know that?"

"No, I didn't. Thank you. We have to get back home now."

More Kimballs! I'd heard enough about them to last me a lifetime!

I walked so fast Florence had to run to keep up with me.

The very first thing we saw as we came back to our house was smoke gushing out of the two kitchen windows. The first thing we heard was Prince Albert barking beside his doghouse, straining at his rope like he'd gone crazy.

"Is it a fire?" screeched Florence.

I cried out, "I don't know, but I don't see any flames."

It wasn't a fire. It was the Old Dickens belching out smoke from every opening it had, and it had plenty. I could see this when I stood on tiptoe to look over a kitchen windowsill. There stood Alec in the middle of the room swatting at smoke while Mama flapped a wet tea towel at the stove.

"Oh, no! They haven't got it working right!" cried Florence beside me. "What'll we do, Marcella?"

"Go in and help get the smoke out. We'll open all the windows and doors. Run around the front and help me."

We ran around the front, but there on our front porch stood a stranger, a tall, pretty lady with a cloud of dark hair piled up in a very stylish pompadour. She wore a pretty white dress with an ivory-colored lace bertha and a wide, white straw hat. Florence and I stopped in our tracks to stare at her.

She smiled down at us. "You would be Marcella, the oldest Abbott girl, and you would be Florence, wouldn't you?"

"Yes, ma'am," I told her. She knew us. *But how?*

"I hear you will be staying on through the year, so I came here to see if you plan to go to school here or in Astoria. I'm the new teacher this year. Is your mother at home?"

I looked behind me. No, this elegant lady couldn't see the smoke from the kitchen yet. I said, "Mama's very busy right now, but I'll go around and ask her to come to the front parlor. What did you say your name is?"

"Miss Kimball. Miss Hester Kimball."

I grabbed hold of the porch post nearest to me to keep from fainting. *Another one?* What a nasty surprise! How could anybody so well-dressed and well-groomed be a Kimball? Was she from some other family with that name?

Wrinkling her nose, she asked, "Do I smell smoke? Good heavens, is your house on fire?"

"Oh, no, ma'am," I told her. I was always very polite to all my teachers because they gave out the grades. "It's our kitchen stove. Mama and Alec, my brother, are trying to get it started."

"Oh, I see." She frowned. "Yes, people who have worked here summers have found that stove difficult."

Florence put in, "Your sister Anna called it the Old Dickens."

Miss Kimball nodded. "If Anna says that's what it is, it is. She seldom minces words. I'll come call on your mother some other time. Well, good-bye, Marcella and Florence. I hope to see you Monday morning." Alas, she was one of the Kimball "natives," even if she didn't seem to be.

As we stood gazing after her, Florence asked me, "Don't the Kimballs ever come to an end?"

"There are eight of them and a father and mother, too. I think they're spread out all over this Peninsula like dandelions going to seed on a lawn. We have to be prepared for them popping up anywhere, anytime. Now let's forget them and get the windows open before the whole house gets full of smoke!"

As Florence went in the front door behind me, she said, "I wish I knew some real good swear words, better than 'drat' and rats,' can't you? I want to curse a lot of things right now."

I knew what she meant. I said, "I bet we'll hear plenty of bad talk from the 'natives' at our new school. Keep your ears open."

"What did you think of the latest Kimball, Marcella?"

As I tugged at a stuck window, I said, "She's pretty and she's really young for a teacher, but that doesn't mean much. The worst, strictest teacher I ever had at St. Helen's Hall was pretty and young, too. Every kid who had her in class used to pray she'd get married and leave. They even brought their big brothers who weren't married around to meet her. When she did get married, we gave her a fancy present, but it wasn't to wish her happiness. It was out of our joy to see the last of her. I think Miss Kimball's going to be strict. Maybe she'll pick on us just because she's a 'native' and we're summer people and she wants to get even with us."

Tugging at the window beside me, Florence said with a nod, "That's the feeling I've got, too."

I found out right away what caused so much smoke in the house. Not realizing it, Mama had used some new-cut wood with moss on its underside. Nothing smoked or smelled so bad as green moss. Campfires at beach picnics had taught me that much, though Mama hadn't seemed to notice. We would have to wait until all that new wood burned up before we could put in seasoned, old wood.

While the Old Dickens went on smoking and rumbling, Florence and I joined Alec and Mama, coughing and flapping at the smoke with wet towels and opening and closing the back door to make a draft.

It took a while to get the smoke out so we could get a good look at one another again. Nobody had soot-blackened faces, but we surely did look frazzled, and I knew we smelled to high heaven of smoke.

"Oh!" Mama sighed. "That was bad."

Florence blurted out, "It was worse than that. We just met our new teacher on the front porch. She didn't come in to meet you because of all the smoke. She's a Kimball, the oldest one of the girls. She didn't leave her calling card."

"What—a Kimball a teacher?" Mama knelt down to pick up one of her tortoiseshell hairpins that had fallen out while she'd run around flapping the towel. "A teacher. Do tell! Well, that is interesting. There seems to be one very good thing that can be said about that family. They must believe in education if one of them has become a teacher. That takes time and effort and willpower. That is a very good sign in any 'native.' "

Well, it certainly didn't seem to me that Mama was much concerned that Miss Kimball had not left her a calling card. In Portland, if a caller came and didn't, she would have been insulted.

In all the troubles of getting settled in and dealing with stoves, we sort of put Miss Kimball out of our minds. On Mama's orders, Alec and Prince Albert and I walked to Mr. Willard's store the day after our teacher had called on us and asked Mrs. Willard to come to our house to show us how to work the Old Dickens. Mama was willing to pay anyone who could teach us how to tame that stove. We all stood around watching the storekeeper's wife set the fire with paper and kindling in the firebox, get it blazing well, and then put firewood on top once it had started. Watching her, I realized I'd been lighting the parlor stove backwards. No wonder it took me so long. The crumpled-up paper came first. Mrs. Willard showed us how to handle the vents and the dampers while Mama wrote down every one of her instructions as she talked.

Mrs. Willard, who was tall with fuzzy yellow hair, seemed to take pity on us. After she'd helped us with the stove, she showed us how to boil dirty dishes and dirty towels on the grates' boiler and rinse the laundry in the sink. Then she showed us how to trim the wicks of the kerosene lamps so they wouldn't smolder and to clean their chimneys of soot. We'd already practiced making beds and sweeping out the sand we tracked into the house.

Just before she left in her buggy, Mrs. Willard asked Mama, "Missus Abbott, what *can* you cook?"

Mama had been hard at work reading in the cookbooks and told her, "Outside of molasses taffy, I believe I can fry several things, like fish and eggs, and

I know now how to roast coffee beans and grind them for the pot, I think, and I can heat up anything that comes in a can. Now that the stove will no longer be a problem to me, I'll try to learn a new dish a day—nothing too fancy, mind you. I will start in the cookbook with *A* and go on to *Z*."

Mrs. Willard only nodded. Then she said, "Well, lean heavy on fresh fish, Missus. I came here from Iowa in my youth. I had plenty to learn about this part of the world. There's a saying here: 'When the tide's out, the table's set.' "

Alec asked, "What does that mean?"

She smiled at him. Most ladies did. Grown-ups found him charming. "It means we eat a lot of clams and oysters and crabs and fish. Missus Abbott, you better learn lots about things that swim. Some you fry. Some you bake and fry. Some you got to boil first. Seafood's the best eating of all here on the Peninsula."

Mama asked, "How do we get these seafoods?"

"Boys who catch them fetch them to the back door to sell in season."

"Do girls catch them, too?" asked Florence.

"You bet. There aren't any faster girls on the ocean beach with a clam shovel than Sarah and Evangeline Kimball."

Them again! I knew what a clam shovel was, but I had no intention of using one.

After Mrs. Willard drove off, Mama told us, "That was money well spent in furthering our housekeeping educations. After all, my cooking and dishwashing and laundry all depend on my mastery of this wretched stove—not to mention having heat in this part of the house in winter. I had never believed a stove could be so important."

Out of the corner of my eye I gave the Old Dickens a quick glance. Mrs. Willard had a way with it, all right. Our coffeepot was boiling, and the laundry in the big copper tub would soon be boiling, too. Of course, we didn't have anything tasty to put into the hot oven, but that would come later.

Suddenly Mama said, "I think I'll attempt a roast beef from the Nahcotta butcher shop for Sunday. I'll put carrots and onions and potatoes in with it. The cookbook recipes for roast beef sound easy. I've already dipped into the *B* section for beef."

I sighed with joy. Roast beef would be wonderful after canned beans and peaches night after night.

Mama went on. "We'll take it slow and easy, my dears, and we'll be just fine. Look forward to Sunday."

## 3

## SCHOOL AND A CHICKEN TO "DRAW"?

But Sunday wasn't fine!

The Old Dickens saw to that.

I'd peeled the potatoes and scraped carrots to go in beside the roast beef, only cutting my finger one time. Florence had peeled onions and cried.

Nobody wanted to handle the chunk of raw beef. It didn't only look fearfully red but was slippery, too. Finally Mama flopped it into the roasting pan with two big forks that she had a hard time pulling out of it afterward.

The stove burned just fine because Mama'd left lots of dampers open. In fact, it burned too well, fast and furious, devouring the firewood Alec stoked it with like a locomotive engineer making steam. And it burned our dinner, too.

When Mama took the roast out, it was half the size it was when it went in, and it was black. My carrots and potatoes and Florence's onions were just greasy black chips.

So I opened up another can of pork and beans for supper while Mama wearily climbed upstairs to lie down with a vinegar-soaked cloth on her forehead.

As the oldest, I figured I'd help her out, so I boiled eggs for breakfast and for our school lunches and got crackers and chocolate biscuits ready to go. I put everything into the kitchen "safe," the cooler box, built into the outside wall with wire mesh around it to keep insects out.

The next morning, we all kissed Mama, said good-bye, picked up our lunches, and left her looking anxiously after us from the back door. Then we patted Prince Albert who, of course, wanted to go with us, and bravely started on our way toward the railroad tracks that went along to the schoolhouse.

Florence said, "I'm scared, Marcella. Maybe the other kids won't be friendly. We never were to them in the summers."

Alec chimed in. "That's right. We never played with them. Maybe they'll laugh at us or fight with us."

I sighed and said, "I don't think Miss Kimball will permit anything like that. Maybe she'll be rough on us, though, because we never went to public schools before and she thinks we think we're too good for that after going to private ones." I turned to walk backward, facing my sister and brother, and said, "I did some deep thinking last night. I have a plan. We'll act real friendly toward Evangeline and Sarah Kimball even if we don't really want to. That could get us in good with their big sister."

Florence complained, "I don't feel like being friendly with them. They're too nosey."

"They're girls. I don't either," said Alec.

I stood firm. "I didn't say we should *really* be friends with them—just pretend to be. It won't be real. It'll be like acting in a play. It could save us a whole lot of trouble."

For a while nobody said anything, then Alec did. "All right, I'll try, but it'll be harder for Florence and you, Marcella. The Kimball girls are your ages. They won't pay much attention to me."

Florence heaved a sigh. "I'll do my best, Marcella."

I soothed her with, "That's the spirit. We'll be the Three Portland Musketeers—one for all and all for one. The Kimball girls won't ever catch on to what we're up to, and neither will their teacher-sister. We'll be so nice butter won't melt in our mouths—even when it's choking us."

Alec growled. "That'll be hard to keep up."

I told him, "Whenever you feel you just can't stand things at school anymore, pull on your earlobe or squeeze your nose like you have to sneeze. The way it'll hurt will remind you not to scream out loud. Florence and I'll do the same, and when we see one of us doing it, the others will smile back to keep your spirits up."

"No," Alec told me. "I'll stick my head in my desk and snarl quietly."

"All right, Alec. Just don't let anybody hear you."

The first person I saw at the little schoolhouse was Sarah Kimball, who was standing on the front porch with the school bell in her hand. She had on a dark-red calico dress with black rickrack trim. I knew she was dressed just right for school here, and we weren't. Florence and I were got up in white dresses with ruffles and pale-colored sashes and long white stockings. Alec wore white knee pants—they were all he had. The Peninsula boys who had started to arrive were mostly wearing blue overalls.

As we went past Sarah, she told us, "In five minutes my sister will yell at me that it's time for school to start and I'll ring the bell for her." She leaned closer to me. "It's her first day ever of teaching. She says she feels like a lion tamer in a cage of new lions fresh from Africa. Better mind your p's and q's around her 'cause she's sort of nervous."

I said, trying to sound friendly, "We're sort of nervous, too. We never went to a one-room school before."

"Oh, heck, Marcy," said Sarah, "you and Flossie and Al will get the hang of it real fast. Hester's barks are worse than her bite."

*Marcy? Flossie? Al?* Nobody in Portland had ever called us those names!

There were twenty-five kids in that one room, sitting two to a desk. I sat among the eighth-graders, at the same desk with Sarah, and Florence was with Evangeline. I was surprised until Sarah told me they'd asked their sister if they could sit with us. They were sure to be teacher's pets from now on—not us.

Miss Kimball was just what I figured she would be—strict. There was no talking or whispering. She made everybody who wasn't a first-grader read out loud and do sums on a blackboard to find out what they did and didn't know. Then we had to spell words for her and give her samples of our penmanship. My handwriting was better than Sarah's, but she outspelled me. Alec pulled at his earlobe so much that Miss Kimball asked him if it ached. After that he did some head ducking into the desk, but that didn't seem to bother her.

At lunchtime we Abbotts ate under one tree while the Kimball girls ate with other Peninsula girls under another one. We couldn't help but notice that other students had real sandwiches made with bread when all we had were crackers and boiled eggs, so I told

Florence and Alec to turn around, and we put our backs to everybody else so we wouldn't be embarrassed. Other kids brought their lunches in old lard buckets. Ours were wrapped up in white damask napkins. We ate with the cloth close to our mouths so nobody could see what we had.

We didn't play tag or baseball at recess the way the others did. We stayed together under our tree and watched. I noticed Sarah and Evangeline Kimball played in all the games even though their sister was the teacher. I also noticed the bigger Peninsula boys and girls would look over at us and grin and whisper together sometimes. What were they up to?

That was when I'd tell Florence and Alec, "Smile back. Don't let them get your nanny. Act friendly. Remember, we're the Three Portland Musketeers."

Finally that first dreadful day was over and we headed for home, walking bone-wearily together. Suddenly, a big older boy came running up from behind us and gave Alec a push that sent him sprawling in the sand.

Before my brother could get up, Evangeline Kimball was on top of the other boy, shaking him while she held him by the collar. She yelled, "You ain't going to fight Al, Jackie! Pick on boys your own size—and don't you dare do it near the school. My sister Hester'll whip the stuffing out of you with a rod. She knows how to do that real good from hitting her brothers."

Evangeline helped Alec rise just as Sarah came running up to dust sand off him.

The three of us politely and smilingly thanked them, then continued on home. I wasn't going to say anything more to them. What had happened was disgraceful. Girls fighting!

To our dismay, Prince Albert wasn't beside or inside his doghouse. We looked all around his little house, getting madder by the second. Had some "native" sneaked up and stolen him? As we hurried toward the kitchen, Mama opened the window and called out, "Don't worry. Albert's in here, children."

Inside? Dogs never went inside our house in Portland. We trooped in the back door and put down the school books Miss Kimball had loaded us down with. There sat our dog on the kitchen floor beside the stove, looking quite pleased with himself. And there was Mama, a bit frazzled-looking because the kitchen was so hot. She'd only catnapped in the kitchen on a chair. She had kept feeding wood into the stove ever since Mrs. Willard had left so it wouldn't go out.

Mama said, "From now on Albert will keep me company inside. This is the first time I have ever been entirely alone in my life. He's to be a house dog. It was so lonely here with all of you gone and no servants in the house. But tell me, how was school? You look weary."

Why should I worry her? I spoke for everybody.

"It was all right. We got along all right." Then, giving Florence and Alec a glance to warn them to let me do the talking, I said, "The Kimballs were nice to us—all of them."

"That's wonderful to hear."

"Did anything happen here?" asked Florence.

"I went to the Nahcotta post office and there was a letter from Papa. He sent us some more money for food, and says he'll send our winter clothing soon. Things are the same for him down in Portland—not good at all." Mama sighed. "On my way to Nahcotta I decided not to try to roast anything for a while again. The butcher didn't have anything to fry in the way of meat that looked good to me, so he suggested a chicken. He said it would be easy to fry, and he even told me how much fat to put into the pan and how much flour to dust it with. I told him to wrap a bird up for me and he did."

I looked around the kitchen but didn't see any chicken. "Where is the chicken, Mama?"

"In a bucket in the pantry. I don't know what to do with it." She frowned. "I told you he gave it to me all wrapped up in butcher's paper. I never saw it in his shop. Well, it's got all its feathers on, you see. Nobody can fry a chicken with feathers all over it. What shall I do with it, I wonder?"

I asked, "What does the cookbook say?"

"It says to 'draw it and singe it.' "

" 'Draw it'?" exclaimed Florence, who was good at art in school in Portland.

"Oh, that doesn't mean to sketch it, Florence," said Mama. "It means to cut it open somewhere on its body and take out all its insides. I never realized a little white chicken could be so much trouble."

I said, "I don't think it is to most people, Mama. Just to us. We don't know how to get the feathers off and what to take out of its insides or what singeing is. I think giblets are the parts you keep to make giblet gravy, but I don't know what a giblet is or what it's supposed to look like once it's out of the bird. Do you know, Mama?"

"I plead guilty," she said, looking unhappy. "I should have asked for a defeathered bird."

I told her, "I think the first thing for us to do is bury the one you bought."

Alec said, "I'll go get the shovel and you get the chicken, Marcella."

Mama had sat down next to the Old Dickens, which was blazing away so hot its top was bright red. She told Alec, "No, let your sisters perform the sad duty for the poor bird. Please go to the woodpile and chop enough firewood for me so this stove will not go out. I'll stay up nights and feed the monster and sleep in the daytime when it lets me. I can read cookbooks by lamplight at night in here." She smiled weakly. "Isn't this an adventure, though?"

43

"No! It's not fun at all," Florence told her on the way to the pantry for the bucket with the chicken in it. "I want to go home to Portland—I want to go home right now, Mama!"

"So do we all," came from Mama. "It doesn't seem we're cut out for wilderness living. But we can't go home. We're going to have to have more help than Mrs. Willard gave us."

I patted her shoulder. "Wait and see! I bet we'll do all right if we all pull together and use our heads."

I planned to use mine. I was going "fishing"—but not in Willapa Bay. I planned to bait a hook for help.

# 4

# HELP AND HORRIBLENESS

The next day at recess the Kimball girls came over to our place under our tree. They plopped down beside us without being invited, and Sarah asked, "How're things going with your ma and Old Dickens, Marcy?"

Aha! A nibble on my hook. I said, "Not so good, Sarah." I'd let her call me Marcy, even though I hated nicknames. I needed her goodwill. I needed her to "bite" on my hook to help us out at home.

Florence told her, "Mama keeps the stove going all the time—day and night. She's scared to let it go out."

Evangeline cried, "Don't she know how to bank a fire at bedtime so it'll go real low all night and catch fire easy with some more kindling in the morning?"

I said, "No. Mrs. Willard showed us how the stove worked, but she didn't stay till dark so we could learn that."

"Oh, my," said Evangeline, looking at Florence. "When does your ma sleep?"

Looking as pitiful as I could, I answered her, "Daytimes, but she has to get up to fix the stove even then." Would Sarah bite?

She "bit." She looked shocked. "Daytime ain't the time to sleep! We'll ask Ma if we can come over to your house after school today and help you with that mean old stove. Anna showed me how it works in case I ever worked summers for you folks. I can handle the Old Dickens."

Aha! Sarah did know! She'd taken my hook in her jaw. I said, "We'd appreciate it if you came back with us today." I added, "We buried a chicken yesterday."

Evangeline "bit" on that. "Are you raisin' chickens already? Was it sick?"

"No. Mama bought one at the butcher's and found out too late that it still had all its feathers on. She wanted to cook it for last night's dinner, but couldn't. The only thing we could think to do was bury it. Prince Albert wouldn't know how to eat meat with feathers on it, either."

"Oh, dear," said Sarah, laughing. Then she added,

46

"We'll ask Ma to let us bring you a fryer today, and we'll show you how to get it ready to cook. Frying is the quickest and easiest. I can fry chickens just fine. My biggest brother Whitney's home today. He'll chop off its head so you won't have to do that."

I heard Florence gulp beside me. We'd never killed a chicken or duck or turkey in our lives.

I said, "I don't think we'll ever raise chickens. We'll pay you for the one you bring us."

Now Alec blurted out, "When you bring the bird, please bring some bread, too. I don't want to eat crackers for weeks while Mama learns how to bake bread in that stove."

I said fast, "We'll pay you for the bread, too, of course."

Then Miss Kimball came out to ring the bell and recess was over. As we went back to the schoolhouse, I whispered to Florence, "I think I'd like to wring Alec's neck a little bit. He's getting friendly too fast with the Kimballs."

She whispered back, "Leave him alone, Marcella. He's doing fine—better than you are."

Now I had a second family neck to wring a little bit. Were she and Alec turning against me? How could they?

The Kimball girls came to our place around three-thirty and brought a sunburned, towheaded, dark-eyed boy named Joel with them. He was about Alec's age, and sat in a desk across from him.

"You know Joel," Sarah told us all. "He lives on the farm next to us. He's a good chicken plucker. He wanted to come. Evangeline didn't make him. That wouldn't be right of us to whip him into coming. Here's your chicken." Saying this, she pulled a limp, speckled, headless chicken out of the gunnysack she was carrying. Then out came three big, delicious-looking loaves of brown-crusted bread. Sandwiches!

Sarah handed the chicken to me, put the bread back in the sack, and went up to our open kitchen windows and yelled, "Mrs. Abbott, if you come out we'll show you how to draw a chicken and pluck it. Joel's a champion chicken plucker in the kid class at county fairs. Bring a washbasin. Don't worry about the stove. If it goes out, I'll come in and fix it for you. And I'll show you how to bank it for the night if you want me to."

Out came Mama in a long, pink-flowered apron that had hung on a hook in the pantry for years. She looked so pretty in it, holding the washbasin. Her hair was not piled up tight but floated around her head in wisps.

Joel went right to work on the bird. He grabbed a handful of feathers and pulled. In a few seconds the air was full of gray-speckled feathers. They went into an old washtub under the clotheslines. When he'd got the chicken down to its skin, he chopped off the yellow, scaly feet with a wood ax. Then he took out a big jackknife and cut open the bird, reached in, and began to pull out parts that were lots of different colors.

He told us, "This here's the gizzard and heart. You can cook 'em for giblets. These are the lungs and bowels and here's the crop. You don't want 'em. This crop can be interestin', though. It'll have little tiny rocks in it. Chickens peck rocks up. You always ought to slit the crop open. Sometimes you find gold nuggets in a crop. Pa knowed a man who did."

Mama said, "What? Gold here on the Peninsula?"

"Nope, down in California it was. There ain't no gold here. Now I'll singe the bird to get off the quills still in it." He pulled matches from his overalls pocket, then took a piece of newspaper from the gunnysack, lit it, and ran it over the bird. After he finished, he put out the fire in the sand. "Now I'll cut it up for you, Missus Abbott, for the skillet." While we all watched, he took the ax again, laid the bird on the chopping block, and hacked it into wings, legs, breasts, backs, and a neck.

As she put the pieces into the washbasin, Sarah told Mama, "Missus Abbott, all you got to do now is wash it, salt and pepper it, roll it in flour, put lard in the pan, and pop it in. Watch it good. Chicken cooks fast. When it's good and brown on the outside, it's ready to eat. What'll you eat with it?"

"Canned beans again, probably," said Alec, who was getting to be a big tattletale.

Sarah nodded. "Why don't you have fried spuds and onions? All you have to do is slice onions and peeled spuds real thin, and put 'em into a skillet with some lard and salt and pepper and keep turning 'em so they don't burn. Stick with it. Spuds take some time."

Mama told her, "That sounds lovely."

"It is," agreed Evangeline. She told Mama, "Our ma heard of a summer lady once who boiled pork chops because she didn't know what else to do with 'em. Her hired girl was sick that day. You always fry or you bake pork chops."

"I will remember that," came from Mama as she took the basin back toward the house. Now she asked, "Wouldn't you all like some chocolate biscuits?"

"We surely all would," declared Evangeline. "Biscuits will go down fine. Ma says we won't take any money for the chicken or the bread. And Joel won't want any for the chicken plucking. After we eat your biscuits, we'll take your bulldog for a walk. It's getting on to sundown so he won't sunburn. We'll take him to our place and show him off to Ma."

I didn't like all this. Things were being taken out of my hands much too soon by the bossy Kimballs. I told Florence, "I'll help Mama with the potatoes. You and Alec can go visiting if you want to."

Sarah grinned at me. "Say, I'll stay here, too, and write down how to bank a fire for the night so you can save on firewood chopping."

So Sarah would be staying? Well, wasn't that what I wanted? Didn't we need her?

After everyone had some chocolate biscuits, I

walked to the back door with her while the others left for their walk. While Sarah went over the workings of the Old Dickens with Mama, I began to peel potatoes. I'd only done it once before—the Sunday we almost had roast beef for supper. After a time, Sarah took the paring knife from me and showed me how fast she could peel and how thin her peelings were where mine were thick. What a smart aleck she was!

After we got the supper going, we sat around the kitchen until the others came back. I noticed Mama seemed to like Sarah. Well! My own mother! I ran out to greet them, happy at getting away from Sarah, wondering how the visit had gone without me there to keep my brother and sister in line.

Prince Albert's tongue was lolling, so I knew he'd been trotted, and that annoyed me. What got to me most, though, was the way Florence and Alec looked. They were barefoot. Their high-top shoes were stuffed with their stockings and hung over their arms by the laces. Florence's pretty sausage curls were a wild tangle like Evangeline's; Alec's hair stood on end like Joel's. They'd all been racing in the dunes and probably running our poor old dog, too.

Florence didn't act one bit guilty. She came right up to me to say, "Mrs. Kimball's pretty and yellow-haired like Evangeline. She's nice. She gave us buttermilk to drink and oatmeal cookies. We saw her stove, the Nickel-Plated Beauty. It isn't new, but it's handsome, and can it ever bake good stuff."

I said, "Isn't that nice, though? You never noticed kitchen stoves before."

"Well, I have good reasons to notice them now, Marcy."

"Marcy"—from my one and only sister! The "natives" had got her. I was about to say, "Call me Marcella," when Sarah spoke up. "We got to get back home now. Thanks a lot for the chocolate biscuits."

Joel added, "Uh-huh, thanks. It's time for my ma to blow the fisherman's horn again. She uses it to let me and my little brothers know it's time to git on home. She gets mad when we tell her we didn't hear it the first time and only come on the second toot. She's already tooted once."

I was shocked. I said, "Why, that's like calling animals! Don't people call hogs to come eat?"

He nodded his towhead. "I guess so, but we don't mind. We can get pretty scattered in the woods and on the sand dunes."

We Abbotts watched our Peninsula neighbors leave. Then I lit into Florence and Alec. "You better wipe that sand off your feet and put on your stockings and shoes before you go inside the house. Mama won't like to see you this way."

Alec turned to Florence. "See! I told you old Marcy would be a spoilsport." The "natives" had got him, too. They surely worked fast.

Florence sighed. "Everybody else runs around barefoot here."

I folded my arms. "I've read that 'barefoot' is also called 'going native'. Is that what you want to do?"

They thought for a long minute. Then, pouting, Alec told me, "The Kimballs and Joel have a lot more fun than we do."

I asked, "Did you see our teacher at the Kimballs', too?"

Florence shook her head. "Not there, but we did meet her coming home from school. She'd stayed to grade papers. Guess what, Marcy! She had her shoes off, too, and was walking in the sand. She said her shoes pinched her toes. She's got nice toes."

I snapped, "Five on each foot, I trust!"

Then I ran for the back door, opened it, and slammed it shut behind me.

"What's the matter, Marcella?" asked Mama, who was rolling a chicken leg in flour.

"It's Florence and Alec. I think they're going to the dogs. Well, I don't plan to."

Mama said, "Oh, you mean by their visiting the Kimballs at their home? I know that isn't the Portland way of doing things. But Sarah is a nice and pretty girl. Their oldest sister is your teacher. You do stick very hard to Portland ways, Marcella. I think you should unbend a bit here. This isn't Oregon, you know. You should try to melt that streak of iron in you that you inherited from your Grandmother Grover."

*Unbend?* And from my own mother! Could it be she

was turning "native," too? It seemed to be catching, like the mumps.

I told Mama, "But Florence and Alec came home barefoot. They said they met Miss Hester on her way to Ocean Park from school, and she was barefoot, too. A teacher going barefoot?"

Mama did a strange thing now. She gave me a look, shook the chicken leg at me, and said with a toss of her head and a laugh, "Why shouldn't she, Marcella? Toes came before slippers. If she doesn't go barefoot in her schoolroom, what business is it of ours what she does outside of it? Can't a lady take off her shoes to ease her feet in private if she wants to? Most likely she didn't expect to meet any of her pupils and shock them. Many's the time in Portland I longed to take off those instruments of torture called shoes. Sometimes I did and walked on the cool, damp grass in the garden. It was delightful. Your father didn't find me any less of a lady for doing that. He liked doing it, too."

I couldn't think of a single thing to say to her. This surely wasn't anything I'd write to my Portland friends. What would they or their mothers think if they knew that Mama had run around half-clad on our lawn!

It was painful enough for me to read Jennie and Jessie Palmer's letters from Portland telling me about their birthday parties in cafes, and about trying out for the school play and going to church socials. They wrote, too, about the silk and taffeta dresses and the hats their mama bought them to wear to autumn goings-on.

No, I had never told them how badly things were going. I didn't want them to feel sorry for us. I always wrote them that we were all enjoying a great adventure, like we were camping out all year long while we "watched the natives." I made it seem like we were North Pole seekers among the Eskimos. Some adventure!

Florence and Alec didn't suffer the way I did. They didn't write letters at all to their Portland friends. When we'd first learned we were staying, they had sent a couple of postcards they'd got at Mr. Willard's store, but they didn't get any answers. Nobody ever replied to postcards, of course. Now they didn't care anymore. They were all caught up with Peninsula kids. Portland, I guessed, was fading in their minds while they ran wild here—or, rather, ran barefoot.

Speaking of feet, it appeared to me that there were always Kimballs underfoot in our lives from then on, from smart-mouth Tom bringing things from the store to Evangeline and Sarah in our kitchen. Florence and Alec welcomed their company. I only tolerated it, although I had to admit Sarah was teaching Mama plenty and Mama was learning fast. Within a week's time she'd more or less tamed the Old Dickens and was cooking roasts and chops. One day she baked skillet bread and the week after that made real yeast bread in the oven. She could sleep nights now, so she had more energy. Chickens didn't faze her anymore. Although she could pluck birds, it was Alec who did it for her, making the feathers fly. He wanted to get to be as good a plucker as his new friend, Joel.

At school things changed, too. Miss Hester changed our seats. She put me in with Evangeline to help her with arithmetic and Florence in with Sarah to get help in spelling. Then we "older girls" could help the younger ones. Because it would be a wise thing to do, I took Evangeline in hand, drilling her hard on multiplication tables, while Sarah forced hard words onto Florence, who had trouble with "ie" and "ei."

As for me, I held myself away from the Kimballs. I wore my shoes and stockings, but I walked home alone now. My brother and sister and the Kimballs and Joel walked ahead and called me "stick-in-the-swamp Marcy." What traitors my kin had turned out to be!

I didn't visit the Kimball house and neither did Mama, but we met Kimball relations in Nahcotta—Mr. and Mrs. Ced Perkins and Dr. Alfred Perkins. Meeting them was mostly by accident—Alec's accident cutting up our fourth chicken. He sliced the back of his hand with the ax. Mama washed the cut and bandaged it, but it became infected, so we had to go to Nahcotta to see the doctor, and Dr. Perkins was the only one there. He lived at the Palace Hotel and Eating House where he had his office, too.

The four of us and Prince Albert walked to Nahcotta, which was a mile away to the east on Willapa Bay. When we came up onto the balcony of the big, white-painted, wooden hotel, Mrs. Rose Perkins, a redheaded little lady, came flying out and cried, "No dogs on my veranda, if you please!"

Right behind her came Anna Kimball. She had on a white apron and cap like a maid's. She grinned at us and told her aunt, "That dog's Prince Albert Abbott. He's a nice clean dog. Let him stay. These are the Abbotts I told you all about, Aunt Rose, the ones who haven't got any money anymore." Now she turned to a yellow-mustached man in a dark gray suit to say, "Uncle Ced, meet the Abbotts. You know all about 'em."

I felt myself fuming once again. Of course they knew! She'd told them everything—even the color of Mama's taffeta petticoats.

Mama said, "How do you do? Florence and Marcella will stay here with our dog while my son and I visit the doctor. Is he in?"

"He's in!" said pointy-nosed Mrs. Perkins. "Go on in, but watch that dog, you two. I don't want my porch pillars chewed on. Come on, Ced, there's work to be done in the pantry." She sniffed and sailed back inside through her big front door. She was a fast walker.

As Mama and Alec went into the doctor's office, Anna Kimball came to the edge of the porch steps. She told us, "Sit down and tell me how you're doing."

"Just fine," I told her without looking at her.

"When's your pa coming to visit you?"

"Thanksgiving probably," said Florence, who shouldn't have told her that. I'd told her not to talk to anybody about our private affairs.

Anna asked, "Is his business going better for him?"

I said, "He's doing just fine." I pinched Florence to keep her quiet. Papa was still deep in money troubles, according to his last letter to us.

Now Anna surprised me by changing the subject. "The rains'll be starting real soon. Have you folks bought any fish oil yet to use on your foul-weather duds? You'd better get it today before it's sold out at the store."

I wrinkled my nose. "Fish oil?"

"You bet. Nothing keeps out the cold and damp like that stuff."

Florence asked, "But how does it smell?"

"Like an old dead fish gone bad, but after a while you don't notice it 'cause everybody else smells of it in wet weather."

I told her, "I don't think we'll need any. We have umbrellas."

She laughed. "Just a little gale here at the beach can turn any umbrella inside out in a second. Oh, well, you'll find out!" And with that she left us to go inside.

We waited until Mama and Alec came out. Mama was smiling. She told us, "The doctor is a most pleasant person, a man of learning. While he cleaned and sewed up Alec's cut, he and I talked about Shakespeare." She patted Alec's shoulder. "He said Alec was a very brave lad."

I asked, "Alec, did getting sewed up hurt badly?"

"You bet your bottom dollar it did. He let me listen to his watch, though, while he was doing it. It plays 'The Blue Danube' waltz. I didn't let out a yelp, though it hurt like hell."

I gasped. Alec had never used that word before. I looked at Mama, expecting her to scold him hard, but all she said was, "Alec, you should use milder language."

"But, Mama, that was what it hurt like!" He turned to me. "I have to come back here on Wednesday after school to have my hand looked at."

"Yes," agreed Mama. Then she added, "We'll go to the store now. Dr. Perkins said we'll be needing fish oil for this winter. I presume it's to take as a winter tonic to ward off colds."

I looked darkly at her. "No, it isn't, Mama. We're to put it on our oilskins so we can smell fishy like everybody else here. It keeps the rain from soaking through. Anna Kimball just told us that."

"Oh, dear, Marcella! Then we'll get fish oil. When in Rome do as the Romans do, huh?"

Mama didn't come with us Wednesday when Alec went to see the doctor again. We walked there directly from school after Miss Hester let us out.

Florence and I went up onto the porch of the hotel and sat in wooden chairs while Alec went inside the office, hoping the doctor would take the stitches out without it hurting too much.

We looked out over gray-blue Willapa Bay where the "natives" fished and gathered oysters. There were white boats on it, bobbing up and down and glistening in the October sunshine. It was surely peaceful—like a museum painting.

Then all at once there was a lot of commotion! A rowboat came scooting up onto the sand and beached itself. A man leaped out of it yelling. His cries brought people away from mending fishing nets and out of stores and cafes and even out of barbershops with lather on their faces.

The man from the boat ran straight up to us. When he came near to the porch, he started to holler, "Dr. Alf, there's been a drowning in the bay!"

We saw the fat, little, yellow-headed, yellow-bearded doctor pop out of his office, pulling on his coat while yelling, "I'll be right there!" A second later he was pounding down the front steps with his black doctor's bag. The hotel owner, Ced Perkins, came behind him at a run.

Now everybody was sprinting for the shore—Florence and me among them, and then Alec, too, holding his unbandaged arm. We watched the men rush to the water's edge. Two big strong ones went into the rowboat and hauled the limp body of a tall, thin man up onto the sand to lay him down.

Dr. Perkins knelt over him, felt his neck, and then straddled him and started to push on his chest. Ced Perkins looked on, biting at his mustache and clenching his fists. Now Anna and Mrs. Perkins were at the water's edge, too, shoving past us and others to get to the doctor's side.

All at once, I heard Anna's high-pitched scream. "It's Whit!"

Whit? Whitney? My memory caught at the name. That was the name of the Kimballs' oldest son, and he was a fisherman! Was this he? I began praying that it wasn't.

Then I heard another cry from behind us, and I turned my head to see Sarah, her long, black hair flying, running toward us. Evangeline was right behind her. They must have heard Anna's screams. Their faces were bone-white as they went past us. The crowd moved back for the two of them, keeping silent now and staring at them.

With her sisters and her aunt, Sarah knelt beside the still man and the doctor working over him.

A man near me asked, "How did it happen?"

Another answered softly, "Whit's foot got caught in a fishing net and he went overboard into the bay. It was a while before anybody could cut him loose underwater and haul him out. He's gone blue. That means it's too late. Doc Perkins is wasting his time."

Eventually the doctor stopped his work. He got off the drowned man, wiped his forehead and eyes, and shook his head.

Alec's scared voice at my elbow said, "That's Sarah and Evangeline's big brother, isn't it?"

I glanced at his hand with the stitches still in it and, wanting to hug him to my chest, said, "We'll go back up to the hotel and wait. Yes, that's their brother." I felt sick.

I didn't want to look at Whitney Kimball, but I had to. There were so many Nahcotta people behind us now that we couldn't get through and head back. We stood with the others while the same two big fishermen carried Whitney past us up to the hotel, one holding his shoulders, the other his knees. His face was blue, his lips a deeper blue, and his black hair a wet, curling cap around his head. All the same I could see he'd been handsome like the rest of his family.

Water kept dripping from his body and falling on the sand path his relatives walked on as they left the beach behind him. Anna's face was covered by a handkerchief, and Evangeline had her head against her aunt's arm. Sarah, her face streaked with tears, looked ahead of her like she was blind. Her uncle's arm was around her to keep her from falling on the slippery sand where the water dripped and dripped.

## 5

# WHERE I NEVER THOUGHT I'D GO

By the time we were home, Florence's face was wet with tears and Alec was swallowing hard. I hadn't cried, but all the same I felt dreadful, like something had hit me in the pit of my stomach. In all our summers at the beach, I hadn't ever set eyes on the oldest of the Kimballs—and now to see him for the first time dead from drowning was a terrible thing, the worst I'd ever seen.

Florence and Alec had met him at the Kimball house the one time they'd taken Prince Albert there to show him to Mrs. Kimball. They told me that while we walked home, and Alec said, "He was nice to us. He promised to whittle a whistle for me, but I suppose he never got around to it."

I told him, "I'm sorry, Alec."

"So am I. I'd have kept it for ever and ever."

Of course, Mama noticed right away how sad-looking we were. Mothers notice things like that faster than they do looks of happiness. She asked, "Why are you crying, Florence? Did somebody in Nahcotta tease you?" She looked at the clean white bandage Dr. Perkins had put on Alec's hand. "Was something seriously wrong with your hand, Alec? Do you have blood poisoning? Oh, God, no!"

I answered for all of us. "No, it hasn't got anything to do with us. Whitney Kimball, the oldest Kimball kid, drowned this afternoon in Willapa Bay. We were there when he was brought ashore in a rowboat. He was dead. Dr. Perkins couldn't help him."

"Oh, my gracious Lord!" said Mama as she sat down all in a heap. "I remember him as a mannerly little boy when I used to come here in my teens, years before I married your father. Whitney had black, curly hair. He used to bring wild strawberries he'd picked to our door and sell them. Oh, this is absolutely terrible! What can we do?"

The three of us sat down in the kitchen, too. The kitchen was where we spent our time now, not in the family parlor as in Portland.

I said, "Mama, I don't know. What do you do in Portland when somebody dies?"

"Your father and I would pay sympathy calls on the families who had lost a relative, and later we would go to the funeral and see to it that there were flowers from us at the cemetery." She sighed deeply. "But mostly we'd do these things out of respect to old people who had passed on and to families we knew well."

I nodded. I remembered Grandmother Grover's funeral and all the mourners in black and the black horses and hearse with black ostrich plumes on its top and heaps of summer flowers on her grave.

Alec asked, "What'll we do for the Kimballs, Mama?"

I said, "Write a letter saying how sorry we are."

Florence shook her head. "Evangeline's my good friend now. She wouldn't like just a letter."

Alec said, "No, that isn't enough. Look at the way they've helped us with the stove and that chicken and other things."

Mama nodded. "Yes, they have been kind to us, kinder than anyone else here. And I haven't gone over yet to Mrs. Kimball to make her acquaintance." She looked at me. "And you haven't visited them either, have you, Marcella?"

"No, Mama, not yet. I'm not so close to Sarah as Florence is to Evangeline." I felt ashamed as I said it.

Mama turned to Alec and my sister and said, "Please go to the kitchen and get Prince Albert and walk him for a while. He needs it. He spends too much time under the stove."

When they had left, Mama turned to me. "Marcella, I know why you are being standoffish with Sarah Kimball. You think they are not our equals, don't you? The Kimballs have been servants, employees, to us in the past, but that's over now. I do not think either Sarah or Evangeline will ever work here for us, even if we regain our money. I can see where you get your attitudes. They came from your father and me and the Grovers and your friends at school. Maybe they fit down in Portland, but all they do here is make you unhappy, darling. We can do for ourselves now—largely thanks to them. The Kimballs have had a dreadful shock. The death of a strong, good, young person is just about the worst shock a family can suffer. The death of an elderly person is expected. The death of a child is a sad, cruel thing." Mama's eyes were suddenly misty with tears. Her voice got softer and deeper. "I feel for Mrs. Kimball in her loss. You don't know it, but your father and I had a dreadful loss, too, and I do not mean money. Marcella, you and Florence and Alec would have had an older brother had he lived."

I gasped. An older brother? I sat fixed to my chair, staring at my mother.

"His name was Bryce. We used your father's mother's maiden name for him. He lived to be almost a year old. Then there was an epidemic of diphtheria and it took him. He would have been fifteen last Valentine's Day."

I breathed. "I never knew! Nobody ever told me."

"No, that's the way your father wanted it." She took her handkerchief from her apron pocket and wiped her eyes. "There's never a day goes by I don't think of him. He had golden curls and such a sweet smile and happy disposition. I was happy you were born a girl. Another boy just then would have been too difficult for your father and me. By the time Alec came along, you and Florence were healthy girls, so it was all right to have a second boy.

"We have to visit Mr. and Mrs. Kimball—all of us, you too." Mama shook her head. "And we ought to take something, but what? We haven't got any flowers in bloom, and I'm not quite up to fancy cookery yet with the Old Dickens."

I said, "How about molasses taffy? You know how to cook it and I know how to pull it."

Her face brightened. "Yes, I could. We've got the sugar and some molasses. Candy might be welcome. I don't think Peninsula people go in much for fancy candies, judging from what I see at the store—mostly peppermint sticks and horehound lozenges."

I said, "We'll dress up like we do going to church in Portland."

"No." Mama held up her hand. "We'll dress properly and plainly. That will be more fitting here. I'll go in my black dress, and you and Alec and Florence in white—and no other colors. We'll attend the funeral, too. When Florence gets back, I'll send her over to the Kimballs' neighbors, the Hogans. I'm sure they will know the time of the funeral. I don't know the customs hereabouts, but I believe it will be tomorrow. We'll plan to go to the Kimball house in the morning." She fixed me with her reddened eyes. "Well, what do you think, Marcella?"

I told her, "You're right, Mama. It's the neighborly thing to do."

I didn't let on to Mama, but after she left to look up the recipe for taffy, I cried—partly for the Kimballs, partly for my lost baby brother, and partly for myself from shame at the way I'd been acting.

The Kimballs had been nice to us. I'd been nasty to them in return. They weren't acting mean or nosey by taking an interest in us. They were looking out for us. Mama and Florence and Alec had seen that—but not me. Not elegant, always-be-right-and-Portland-proper Marcella.

Dragging my feet, I went out to sit on the back steps to wait for my sister and brother. While I waited alone, I thought about the Kimballs and about myself. Well, they weren't about to change, and why should they? This was their part of the country, not mine. So I would have to do the changing and do it now. Mama was right as rain about that.

I was still crying a little when Florence and Alec came up with a panting Prince Albert. After Alec let him inside to go find Mama, I asked them to sit down beside me on the steps. I told them what Mama had told me about little Bryce, and Florence, who'd been red-eyed during my telling, began to cry again. Alec didn't cry. He gulped over and over again and wiped his nose.

Finally he asked me, "Did Mama say we're going to the funeral?"

I nodded. "Yes, she said we will."

Florence sniffled and told me, "We met Joel on the sand dunes. He told us the funeral is tomorrow."

I said, "We'll be taking molasses taffy to the Kimball house."

Florence said, "That'll be a good thing to give. Evangeline told me once she's never tasted taffy. Can we let Sarah and Evangeline know about Bryce?"

I shook my head. "No, not yet. They've got sadness enough of their own right now."

Mama and the three of us walked to the Kimball house the next morning in a light rain. Alec carried our pale-brown taffy in a candy box. We went over tall sand dunes and planks laid in the sand for wagons to pass over and a little forest of dark evergreens. Judging from the buggies and wagons in front of the Kimball picket fence, lots of folks were there before us. A stream of people were going in and out of the house. The women and girls carried baskets which were probably full of food, and the men walked with their hands clasped behind them. Not everybody had on black clothes, but everybody wore something dark.

Miss Hester opened the front door of the big silvery-gray house. We could tell that she'd been weeping. She looked surprised, then smiled as she saw us. She said, "Thank you for coming."

Alec gave her the candy box with the words, "Here's some taffy for you. We made it out of molasses. Mama did. The rest of us pulled it."

"Thank you, Alexander."

I said, "I brought Sarah a book and Florence brought Evangeline her blue hair ribbons."

"Thank you. You'll find my sisters in the parlor with the rest of the family. My mother and father are there, too."

We went into a room with the draperies pulled so it was lit by lamp and candles. Washtubs full of dark red dahlias and purple asters filled the corners. Except for chairs along one long wall, there was no furniture. A wooden coffin sat on top of three sawhorses in the middle of the room. It was closed and a white candle in a brass holder burned at one end of it. A bunch of lavender strawflowers lay next to it.

The Kimball girls, all in dark dresses, were sitting on the chairs—Sarah, Evangeline, Anna, and one I didn't know, who had to be Clarrie. Tom and Cameron Kimball wore dark suits with long trousers. Mr. and Mrs. Kimball stood beside the coffin with Mr. and Mrs. Perkins from the hotel. Mr. Kimball had gray-streaked black hair and a beard. Mrs. Kimball resembled her hotelkeeper sister, though her hair was more yellow than red.

Sarah stood up as I went over to her. I hugged her while Florence hugged Evangeline, and Alec shook hands with the Kimball young men. As Mama walked up to the parents and said something in a low voice to both of them, I handed Sarah my Sherlock Holmes book. It was one of my favorites. I told her, "This is for you. It's got lots of exciting things happening in it."

"Thank you, Marcy, very much," Sarah replied with a little smile.

Then we filed past Whit's coffin and went back out by Miss Hester. I didn't dare hug her because she was a teacher, but all us Abbotts shook her hand as we went by. It was cold as an icicle.

At one o'clock we went to the funeral in the cemetery. We stood among the Peninsula people while the service was read by a Nahcotta minister. Then the coffin was lowered into a grave lined with pine-tree boughs so the brown dirt couldn't be seen. We all sang "Abide With Me," a hymn we knew from Portland, and watched as each of the Kimballs picked up a clod of earth and let it fall onto the casket. I hated the dull, thumping sounds the dirt made.

When the service was over, most of the people went back to eat a funeral dinner, but not us. Mama felt that as outlanders from Portland, we shouldn't push ourselves onto Peninsula people too fast and risk over-doing our welcome. So we headed for home, feeling like outsiders, walking quietly two by two in the rain.

Suddenly Florence said, "I sure miss Papa right now!"

That was just what I'd been thinking, too. We weren't really a family without him. Families should be all together at things like weddings and christenings, and especially at funerals.

# 6

# THE LADY
# FROM THE SEA

In the days that followed, I worked hard at making a friend of Sarah Kimball. She didn't tell me to go away as I'd been afraid she might. Though she was quieter than usual, she acted as she always had toward me. Now I sought her out—hunted her up at recess and noon. I sat with her where we could find a dry place and traded part of my corned beef sandwiches and boiled eggs for her roast beef and chicken ones. I loaned her an Alexandre Dumas book, my very favorite, and when she hugged me gratefully, I hugged her back. She smelled nice—not of eau de cologne, but of the pine tar soap she used to wash her hair.

Florence and I were careful with the Kimball sisters because we could tell they were grieving hard. When they wanted to talk we did, and when they walked home quiet with us we were quiet, too.

October went by with lots of rain and Papa writing us twice a week and sending Mama money for food. He was doing "well enough" down in Portland—and "good news," he hoped to be with us in Ocean Park for Thanksgiving!

The month of November blew in—that was the only way to put it. It came with a northeast wind off the Pacific Ocean and dark gray skies and fast-moving black clouds that dumped drizzling rain on us. Sarah and Evangeline said it was time for fish oil, so they showed us how to smear it on our yellow foul-weather hats and long coats to make them more waterproof. Our slickers smelled so bad that Prince Albert wouldn't even come out from under the Old Dickens when we wore them. From then on, Mama made us take our oilskins off the minute we got home and hang them on the nails she had driven into the back-porch wall—even before we were allowed into the kitchen.

Everybody at school wore fish-oiled coats. With the school's Franklin stove lit, we all stank so bad you could hardly get your breath until you got used to the odor by ten o'clock. After that, the fresh outside air at recess smelled strange.

By now Mama had also learned how to use Grandmother Grover's sewing machine. She'd bought cloth and patterns at the Nahcotta cloth store, and while we studied at night, her foot worked the treadle back and forth as she sewed calico dresses for Florence and me and gingham shirts for Alec. Papa had shipped us our winter clothes, but what use did Florence and I have for taffeta dresses or dark blue or green velvet coats with white fur trimmings, or Alec for black velveteen knee britches? He insisted on wearing overalls now, like the Peninsula boys.

On the tenth of November, a Friday night, the first storm of the winter came roaring in. What a horrible night that was! In all the times I'd been at the beach, I'd never known anything like it. Flashes of lightning zigzagged across the sky. Thunder growled. Windows groaned in their frames. Shingles blew off the roof. The Old Dickens and the parlor stove howled as the gale winds blew down their stovepipes. Our trees tossed and swayed, and rain pounded down like arrows on our porches.

We huddled around the cozy, warm Old Dickens with the kerosene lamps flickering. We'd never known anything like this in Portland. It scared us half out of our wits and made us long even more for Papa. The storm went on all night long, blowing wet, icy sand against the house until the storm moved inland at dawn.

All was finally calm, but it was a weird sort of calm that made a person feel like she'd gone through a big fight or had been sick. Nobody had got much sleep. Mama had kept us all downstairs in the kitchen for fear the roof above our second-story bedrooms would blow off. Alec, being manly, said it wouldn't, and it didn't.

The after-dawn sky was a washed-out, pale blue-gray with strange-looking white clouds, very high up and all gathered together. Just as we finished our breakfast oatmeal, we heard a shout from outside, followed by the nickering of a horse.

I ran to the kitchen window to look outside and see who was coming. It was Sarah and Evangeline, each of them astride one of their big, old white workhorses.

Sarah saw me and called, "Hey, come on out, and we'll ride down to the beach and see what the storm's been up to this time!"

Mama said we could go, but to make sure to dress warmly and not to get into any trouble. She had surely changed. She wouldn't have let us go six months ago, and, of course, no "native" would have invited us anywhere anyway! We were becoming accepted on the Peninsula. As I put on my red knit cap and scarf, I had to admit that I liked that. I'd changed, too, in spite of myself.

Sarah motioned to me to get up behind her on her

horse, and Florence and Alec piled on behind Evangeline. Then off we went at a trot.

Turning her head, Sarah told me, "There'll be other folks on the beach looking for what the storm could have blown ashore. Sometimes cargo on the decks of ships gets washed overboard. That's how we got our red plush sofa and golden oak table."

I said, "They're nice pieces of furniture." Then I said, "You must miss your brother a lot."

"We sure do—all of us. You can't imagine what it's like. We keep expecting him to come in the back door."

I said, "I don't know what it's like, but we had a baby brother who died before I was born. Mama told me about him the day your brother died. I never knew about him before."

Sarah nodded. "My folks say dying's a thing that happens to people of all ages. Ma says it's a remarkable thing and something to be very thankful for that the rest of us Kimballs are so strong. It ain't that way in every family here. Lots of folks on the Peninsula have lost babies and little kids to sicknesses. If it ain't that, it's accidents. Dr. Alf says someday maybe things will be better. Diphtheria and pneumonia won't be a threat when doctors find out more. He says they've already licked smallpox. He vaccinated all of us." She spoke to the horse now that we were out on the plank road through the dunes. "Come on, Prince. Show how fast you can trot."

I said, feeling a little jealous, "I wish we still had a horse. We had two to pull our carriage in Portland, and a pony, too."

"I know you did, Marcy. Anna told me your pa had to sell them. I'm sure sorry."

So there had been more listening at our kitchen door! But all I said now was, "Thank you, Sarah. It hurts to think about Dandy. Oh, well, as the French say, 'C'est la vie.' 'That's life.' I could teach you some French if you want me to."

She looked back at me again. "I don't think so, Marcy. Anyway, not right now. Who'd I talk French with here at the beach? Where do you talk it down in Portland?"

"In elegant French cafes—that's the only place." I had to laugh when I said that. There and in my French class at school. Nobody else in my family could speak it. Mama had forgotten hers.

"Anyhow," Sarah went on, "I think I'd rather take Latin in high school. I want to be a nurse and Dr. Alf says I'll need Latin. What do you want to be when you grow up, Marcy?"

*Be?* That stopped me. All I'd ever expected to be was somebody's wife, a rich man's wife, like Mama. I fibbed. "I haven't made up my mind yet." Actually, a married lady wasn't all I wanted to be, now that I'd come to think about it. I could tell that was what Mama thought now, too. She didn't feel that being a society lady was enough anymore.

The sand beyond the plank road was hard-packed from last night's rain and crunched like sugar under Prince's big hooves. There was still some wind off the sea, and it blew dirty, yellow foam into our faces in cold gusts.

And then we were at the top of a very long beach that stretched north and south as far as my eyes could see. The tide was out, and the tall breakers crashing in yellowish froth on the dark sand were far away. Beyond them the deep, deep gray ocean heaved like a pot just getting ready to boil.

Sarah called out to Evangeline, "We'll race you to the driftwood line," and nudged Prince with her heels.

I wouldn't have thought Sarah's horse could get up a canter, but he did. He and Evangeline's horse, Maude, trotted along side by side until we got to where logs and tree branches and other things had been washed up onto the shore. There was a forest of tangled-up, sun-bleached wood here, wet and darker than usual because of the rain. Mixed in were lots of long, slimy brown strands of kelp that had been torn up from the ocean's bottom by the storm. Over our heads the white seagulls flew around, screeching at us and at each other and swooping down to the kelp for what they could find in it to eat.

Farther down the beach, toward the mouth of the Columbia River, we could see the tiny, dark figures of people at the shoreline or up in the driftwood. But where we were, there was no one but us.

79

Sarah told me, "Some of the men down there are surfmen from the Klipsan Beach Station. They patrol the beach looking for sailors washed overboard in gales." I felt her shiver and hugged her tighter around the waist. She was thinking of her brother Whitney, I knew.

I asked, "There weren't any ships wrecked last night, were there?"

"Not that we heard about at our house. If a ship's spotted coming ashore, Peninsula men come to get Pa to go out with them to the waterline. They all carry lanterns and ropes. The lanterns are so the people on board the ship can see where the land is. Years ago, Peninsula men used to tie themselves to a rope that other men on shore held onto. They'd swim out to a wreck and grab folks off it, then get hauled back in. But the Lifesaving Service usually does that nowadays. Pa swam out a couple of times, and Uncle Ced, too. But mostly he and the other men just swing lanterns now." Sarah pulled back on Prince's reins and slowed him to a walk. Then she leaned over to pat his neck. "That's just fine, Prince. You're a good horse."

He pricked his ears forward, as if he liked what she'd said. But then, suddenly, he jerked on the reins, raised his big head, nickered, and started to rise up on his hind legs. I hung on to Sarah for dear life as he plunged and kicked.

"What's the matter, boy?" she called out to him.

Leaving me, she slid off him and held him by the bridle, patting his nose. She looked worried.

She stared up at me and said, "Something's wrong!" She turned to Evangeline and shouted, "Halt Maude. *Listen!* Be quiet." Her voice got softer now. "I wish we had brought our dog Red with us. Prince knows something. Maybe he heard a noise. Listen, everybody."

We all kept quiet, listening. Then Prince nickered again and swung his hindquarters. When it was silent again, I heard something. It was a faint sound, like a baby whimpering or a cat mewing.

Sarah told me, "Marcy, I'll give you the reins now. Take Prince over to Evangeline. There's something over there in the timber and seaweed. Can you hear it?"

"Yes. What're you going to do?"

"Go see what it is. What else?"

"No, Sarah. You aren't going alone! Wait and I'll come with you." I took Prince's reins from her and trotted him over to Maude to give his reins to Evangeline. Then I slid down and ran back to Sarah, who had picked up two stout pieces of driftwood. She gave me one of them with the words, "If you have to use this, use it. Maybe it's something wild and dangerous in there—like a sea lion. They bite."

We went forward cautiously, guided by the sounds, to a big pile of kelp.

"Whatever it is, that's where it is," I whispered to Sarah.

"It sure is." All at once she let out a yell that made me jump. "Hey, you in there! Get outa there right now."

Nothing ran out of the brown slimy mass or even moved in it, but after a few seconds the noise came again.

I said, "I think something's hurt in there."

"I guess so. Let's go in and see."

Sarah and I went into the kelp, brushing it apart with our free hands and kicking the slick strands away with our feet. They looked like big brown snakes. Ugh!

The first things we saw in the kelp were two feet, very white, bare ones. It was a *person* in there! Now we really tore at the kelp, getting it out of our way. We worked from the feet on up. First we saw some white cloth with a rope around it—the rope was tied around the person's legs. Then we got up to the waist and saw more white cloth and more rope, then to the shoulders, which also were tied up. Tied up? *Why?*

As I worked, I told the person, "It's all right. We're here. We won't hurt you. You'll be just fine. We'll get you loose."

It was Sarah who uncovered the person's face. It was a young woman. She was beautiful, so beautiful, in fact, that she made me catch my breath and think of sleeping princesses and damsels in deep distress. Her braided hair was long and pale gold, and her eyebrows and lashes were dark. Her face looked like it had been carved out of snow, it was so white. Her eyes were closed very tight, and she moved her head from side to side, whimpering.

I asked, "Oh, Sarah, who did this to her? Who tried to kill her by tying her up like that and burying her in the kelp?"

Sarah gave me an exasperated look. "Nobody tried to kill her, silly. Somebody saved her life. Look at what she's tied to. It's a ship's mast."

A mast? Yes, there was a wooden pole beneath her, and the ropes went around that, too.

Sarah went on. "Sailors do that when a ship founders in a storm at sea. They tie people to masts to float ashore. There must have been a wreck last night nobody heard about. That can happen."

The two of us had been on our knees in the kelp. Now Sarah helped me up. She told me, "You stay here with the washed-up lady, Marcy. Flossie and Al can stay, too."

I asked, "What're you going to do?"

"Ride Prince fast as I can to Nahcotta and get Dr. Alf. I'm going to tell my sister to gallop Maude home and get Pa to hitch up the wagon and come down here with it. Dr. Alf may send this pale lady home for Ma to nurse. He's done that before. When there are wrecks, Peninsula folks take in sailors who are hurt." She reached into the pocket of the boy's plaid jacket she wore, took out a bone-handled knife, and gave it to me. "Cut her loose while we're gone. Get the lady to open her eyes if you can. Don't scare her, though."

I told her, "I know better than to do that. It must have been terrible for her in that water. It's so cold and the surf's so strong, she could have drowned."

Sarah gave me a sad look that told me she was thinking again of her drowned brother, and I was sorry for my words. She didn't say anything to me, though, but left at a run. The Kimball girls didn't waste any time. Sarah and Prince took off in one direction, Evangeline and Maude in the other.

Florence and Alec came to stand over the woman and just stared and stared. I told them what Sarah said had probably happened. Then I added, "The shipwreck must have happened at night because she's got on a nightgown." At least it looked like a nightgown to me. It was white cloth, cross-stitched with embroidery at the collar and cuffs.

I said, "I'm going to cut her loose," and unfolded Sarah's jackknife.

The lady from the sea had stopped whimpering by this time, and Florence whispered, "She doesn't look very much alive."

"Well, she is; look at her chest, Florence. It's moving up and down, so she's breathing."

Just then the lady coughed, and Alec and Florence leaped backward.

I told them, "There! Dead people don't cough!"

I started sawing through the wet ropes at the lady's shoulders. It wasn't easy work. The rope was strong.

Then I freed her at the waist and knees. When I finished, I said, "Let's clean off a place in the sand for her so we can get her off the hard wood mast."

Working together, we pushed kelp and moved pieces of driftwood aside until there was a clear, sandy space next to the lady. Then we lifted her together and laid her down.

The minute she felt herself being lifted, the woman screamed out loud. But when she felt the sand under her, she rose up on her elbows for an instant and fell straight back.

"Golly!" said Florence. "She's swooned!"

I corrected her. "Swooning is what ladies do in books. In real life they faint."

Alec asked, "What'll we do now, Marcy?"

"We wait for Dr. Perkins or Mr. Kimball to show up. When a lady faints, you're supposed to chafe her hands, so we can do that, I guess."

Alec volunteered, "Or we could throw some water on her."

That was just like my brother. I scolded him, "She's had too much water already!" I was chafing her hands, rubbing them hard now because they were very cold and bluish from the water.

As I rubbed, Alec took off his coat and put it over the lady's shoulders. I told him, "That's fine, Alec. Your sweater's heavy enough for you right now. I'm sure Mr. Kimball and the doctor will bring blankets to warm her up."

Florence asked, "Did she tell you and Sarah who she is? What ship did she come from?"

"She never said a word. All she did was whimper and scream that one time. I think maybe she's too weak to talk to us."

Alec asked, "Did she scream because she was afraid of us?"

"I don't know. She never looked at Sarah and me once. Come on. Sit down beside me while we wait. We'll sit close around her to keep the wind off her as much as we can. Give her your jacket, Florence, and I'll give her mine. Alec, you chafe her feet. Florence, you can stroke her brow to soothe her the way they always do in books."

"She's surely pretty," said Florence after a while. "She looks like the fairy-tale Snow Queen lying there, doesn't she?"

"Yes, she does," I agreed, "or like a princess from the sea."

And so we went on chafing and soothing until we heard the sound of hoofbeats. I got up to see Prince with Sarah on him pounding toward us, with the Palace Hotel's wagon and Dr. Alf's buggy coming along fast behind her.

Just at that moment, the lady from the sea mumbled one word: "Mott."

Mott? What could that mean?

# WHO IS SHE?

Just before they all got up to us, Alec said, "Hey, we ought to have Prince Albert along with a keg of brandy around his neck."

I gave him the look I'd seen plenty of girls give little brothers and told him, "Those are Saint Bernard dogs in the Swiss Alps, not English bulldogs on the beach."

He wasn't fazed. "Well, maybe brandy would help her. Papa says brandy helps most everything that goes wrong with grown-ups."

Florence, who was still kneeling beside the lady

from the sea, said, "What do you suppose 'mott' means? I used to know a girl in Portland named that."

I said, "Then maybe it's her last name. What else could it be?"

By this time, Sarah and Prince, the hotel wagon, and the doctor's buggy had come up to us.

Dr. Alf got down out of the buggy like he was younger than he appeared to be. Ced Perkins held his team and the doctor's horse's reins. Sarah slid down off Prince and ran along beside the doctor, keeping up with his long strides.

I called out to him, "She's over here! We cut her loose from the mast."

He didn't pay any heed to us. He went past us, dropped to his knees on the wet sand, took a stethoscope out of his coat pocket, and put it around his neck. He felt the sides of the pale lady's neck, then slipped the end of the stethoscope into the front of her nightgown. All of us held our breaths.

All at once he stopped listening to her chest, got up, and said, "I can hear a heartbeat, but I can also hear water in her lungs." He called out as he removed our coats and jackets from her and laid them on the sand, "Ced, bring the blankets from the wagon." He spoke to Alec, "You, my lad, go hold the hotel horses and my Rosinante so my brother can help me here."

I asked, "What can we do?"

"First of all, keep out of the way. Stand back."

I said, "We chafed her hands and feet."

"That did no harm, but you should not have moved her once you cut her loose. That could have harmed her."

I said, "She screamed when we did. I'm sure sorry."

Dr. Perkins shook his head, but didn't scold me.

As Alec ran to the wagon, Florence asked the doctor, "Is she going to die?" A glance at Sarah stopped the rest of her question.

"I don't know. You couldn't have known not to move her, children. We'll try to save her. Did she say who she was?"

I told him, "All she said was 'mott'."

"Mott?" He shook his head. When his brother was there to help him move the lady into a blanket, he asked, "Ced, have you ever heard of any people named Mott in these parts?"

"No, Alf, not any I ever heard of." I saw how Ced Perkins was eyeing the mast. As he and the doctor lifted the lady in the blanket, he said slowly, "Offhand I'd say that's a schooner's mast. We had us a riproarer of a gale last night. It's my guess this poor girl came off a ship that went down at sea."

We followed the two men to the wagon. Sarah lowered its tailgate and they set the lady down in a nest of blankets and sacks. Dr. Alf got up beside her, and Alec handed the horse's reins to Ced Perkins after the man finished tying the doctor's horse to the rear of the wagon. A moment later they were headed east to Nahcotta.

I asked Sarah, "Where'll the lady from the sea stay?"

"At the hotel. That's where she'll get the best nursing. In a big wreck, sailors who aren't hurt too bad are boarded in people's houses all over, like I told you. But real sick ones go to the hotel or the Astoria hospital. Aunt Rose and my sister Anna will take good care of the washed-up lady. Dr. Alf'll show 'em how." All at once Sarah turned around and said, "Pa's coming with our wagon now."

"There isn't anything for him to do now that the lady's gone."

Sarah shook her head. "Yes, there is, Marcy. Pa will go looking for pieces of the lady's ship in case it broke and floated ashore. Sometimes sea chests wash up, too. They can have ship's papers in them. If the hull comes ashore, we may find the name of the ship painted on it."

I told her, "We heard the lady say 'mott'."

"What does that mean?"

"I don't know."

"Did she open her eyes, Marcy?"

"Not that I ever saw."

Florence spoke up softly. "I saw her open them just one time, but maybe she didn't even see me—not really. She's got the strangest-color eyes I ever saw." She took in a deep breath. "With that pale yellow hair and white skin, a person would expect her to have blue eyes, but hers are yellow. She's got golden eyes."

"Eyes that are gold-colored?" echoed Sarah. "Nobody's got eyes like that."

"Well, she has!" insisted Florence.

I believed her. Florence almost never fibbed. But golden eyes? I felt a chill run down my spine and run back up again. This was getting more and more like a fairy tale all the time.

When Mr. Kimball and Evangeline reached us, Sarah, Alec, Florence, and I ran to meet them and told them about the doctor and Mr. Perkins having taken the lady from the sea away with them. When we had finished, Mr. Kimball chewed hard on his mustaches a bit and told us, "I'm going to comb the beach for wreckage. You kids mount up on Prince and Maude and go north to see what you can find. I'll go south with the wagon. Sarah, you and Evangeline know what to look for."

"Sure, Pa," came from Sarah, "flotsam!" She turned to us. "Come on, you Abbotts, let's get aboard our horses and comb the beach. How long'll your ma let you stay out with us?"

I told her, "Till lunchtime for sure, but we'd better be home by then or she'll start to worry. I know how she is."

Sarah nodded. "It's early. We can cover quite a stretch of beach before then even if we walk the horses. We have to look real sharp in the kelp and driftwood for new-looking timber. It won't be gray like driftwood is. Look for paint and colors."

I asked, "Have you done this before?"

"Uh-huh. We always look for washed-up stuff after a big storm." She gave me a strange look. "One time long ago Pa found a sailor who was washed overboard. He wasn't so lucky as the lady we just found. Maybe we'll find somebody else off her ship who isn't lucky. We could, you know. She might not be the only one who's washed ashore."

I said, "I sure hope we won't find anybody. What if we do?"

"I go hunt for Pa while you stay beside whoever we find. Can you do it?"

I looked her straight in the eyes and said, "Yes, Sarah, we can do it."

The five of us hunted and hunted on the shore, now and then getting off the horses and looking in tangled-up piles of kelp while gulls dived at us. Whenever we met other people combing the beach, Sarah told them about the washed-up lady and asked them to look for flotsam, too.

In spite of all that hunting, we didn't find anything—neither wood from a new wreck nor pieces of furniture nor torn-up canvas sails nor barrels. How discouraging!

The Kimballs took us home close to noon. Once we got off the white horses, they headed for their house at a trot. Florence, Alec, and I ran inside to tell Mama everything that had happened that morning.

She listened to our tale over our soup-and-sandwich

lunch and exclaimed, "That's a most remarkable story—a young girl with yellow eyes is cast up from the sea and comes ashore. It's very romantic."

Florence said, "Her eyes aren't yellow. They're *golden*."

Mama smiled at my sister, then murmured, "So the men think she's from a ship that went down at sea and that all the crew aboard were lost in the ocean?"

I said, "Yes, unless Mr. Kimball or some other men find something or somebody. Sarah said wrecks happen here a lot."

"Yes, they do. This part of the West Coast is called the Graveyard of Ships—not a pretty name for such an attractive place. That's because of the shifting sandbars and racing tides. And you say the girl's name is Mott. That's not a particularly common name, but I've heard it before. It's an East Coast name, as I recall. She must be American, then." She sighed. "Lord only knows where her ship was headed or where it came from—Seattle, San Francisco, San Pedro, Portland. There are so many ports on this coast, you know. She could even have come from just above this peninsula—above Oysterville, I mean. Well, as soon as she recovers a bit, she'll tell Dr. Perkins all about herself and what happened, I'm sure."

Florence's face was somber. "*If* she gets well enough, Mama. Dr. Perkins said he'd try to save her. He didn't say that he could for sure. He said he heard noises in her chest."

Mama nodded. "That would be seawater. Well, children, you all tried to help her. You did what you could, and that makes me proud of you. It must have been frightening for you."

I said, "It was. It scared Sarah and me at first when we heard her whimpering in all that kelp, so we got sticks before we came up to her. We were afraid of what might have been there—maybe a wild sea lion, Sarah said."

"All sea lions are wild, Marcy," scoffed Alec.

Mama scolded him. "Hush, son. Marcella did a brave thing, and so did Sarah. I'm proud of both of you girls, and I'm sure Mr. and Mrs. Kimball will be, too. I will write your father all about this tonight."

"I wonder when we'll find out something about her," I said with a sigh. I hoped it would be soon.

As it turned out, there was news on Monday morning, and we Abbotts heard about it even before school started. Sarah talked first. "Anna came home yesterday for our Sunday dinner. Anna said she and Aunt Rose Perkins are nursing the lady night and day. She's got a busted left leg. Dr. Alf set it."

Evangeline added, "She's got pneumonia, too."

Sarah added, "Yes, but it isn't the galloping kind yet. That gets worse and worse real fast. She's in bed all covered up and surrounded with hot-water bottles and oven-heated bricks wrapped in flannel. Dr. Alf says she's got a high fever and that's bad. She's going to have to have a 'crisis.' "

I knew what that was—the point where a person who has pneumonia either gets better or dies. I asked, "Has she said anything?"

Evangeline shook her head. "Anna says all she says is 'mott'. Anna says she mumbles other things, but nobody can catch what she's saying."

Florence asked, "Did she open her eyes again?"

Sarah answered, "Anna says she did, and they're yellow and real strange—like a cat's eye color."

Florence said flatly, "They're pure golden, but not like a cat's. I know gold when I see it."

Alec asked, "When can we go visit her? After all, we found her. We have a right to see her, haven't we?"

Sarah shook her head. "Nobody goes in her room but Dr. Alf or Aunt Rose or Anna. When the lady can have visitors, we'll tell you."

I asked, "Do you know anything about her? Did your father find any parts of a new wreck on the beach?"

"Not one single scrap of wood or anything else." Sarah shook her head again. "After Aunt Rose dressed the lady in one of her own nightgowns, she looked at the one the lady had come ashore in. It was plain white cotton with a little bit of white cross-stitch hand-embroidering on the collar and cuffs. It was all homemade—she could tell. Dr. Alf says, except for the busted leg and bruises from the surf and mast and burns from the rope she was tied up with, there wasn't one mark or scar on her. He thinks she's about twenty years old. He looked inside her mouth. He says she never went to a dentist. Her teeth don't have any fillings, and she'd never had even one pulled out. He said they're just perfect."

My tongue went to the side of my jaw where a dentist had worked on me last year in Portland. I envied the lady her perfect teeth. Dentists can hurt.

Sarah went on. "So, there's no way of finding out who the washed-up lady is until she's ready to tell us. Uncle Ced checked with the Lifesaving Service at Klipsan Beach. They've been on the telegraph all along the coast. There were a couple of ships that got in trouble in that storm, but they got into port or rode the gale out all right. There aren't any ships missing that they've heard of, and no ship out in the storm saw another one sinking. My sister Hester says we'll just have to be patient and bide our time. Isn't it exciting, Marcy? It's just about the most mysterious thing that has ever happened here!"

Before I could nod my head in agreement, Sarah went on. "Hey, I forgot to tell you about the ropes! Uncle Ced went back to the mast and got the pieces of rope. He brought them back to the hotel and looked at them real close. He said there's something strange about them. It isn't rope that we use here on the Peninsula at all. It's real tightly coiled cloth with wax all over it. He says he never saw any rope or cord like it before. It's awful strong, and the lady was tied on with sailors' knots, old-time deep-water sailors' knots."

Just as Miss Hester called her to ring the bell to start school, Sarah whispered to me, "Golly, Marcy, what if that mast hadn't floated the way it did? The poor lady would have been face-down in the water. Uncle Ced noticed that there'd been a crosspiece at the top of the mast, but it had busted off in the sea. Lordy knows when or where—but the lady always floated face-up."

# 8
# PAPA AND "GOLDEN EYES"

Papa was coming up for Thanksgiving, and were we ever excited! The way we acted, it was as if we hadn't seen him in years. We all went to the railroad depot to meet him, Prince Albert, too, and we all rushed forward to grab him and kiss him. I cried. So did Florence. After he had hugged and kissed all of us and patted Prince Albert, we walked home together in the rain, a family all together once more!

Though I didn't say so, it was my opinion that Papa didn't look so good. I asked if I could carry his valise for him and he let me. He was thinner and gray in the face and tired-looking. He surely was working hard and maybe not eating properly. Well, we'd feed him up and we'd see to it he got some rest and exercise before he had to go back Sunday afternoon.

He admired our looks. He told Mama, "All this ocean air makes you prettier than ever, Nelline. I've never seen the children look so healthy. You've managed well here, I see."

"Why, thank you, Henry." She laughed. "We're going to show you how we've managed. You can sit and watch us do things we could never have done three months ago."

And how we showed him! He exclaimed over how we all could boil laundry and sweep and dust, and he could barely believe what Mama had sewn on the sewing machine. He watched Alec chop wood and pluck and draw the Thanksgiving dinner wild goose. Joel's father had shot a goose and given it to us as a present. Papa marveled as Mama stuffed it with sauerkraut and baked it along with pumpkin and apple and mince pies and handled the Old Dickens, getting it to behave just like a lion tamer tames a lion. He was impressed at the long curlicues Florence's and my paring knives made of the apple and potato skins we peeled. And he greatly admired the Thanksgiving table we had set with a white cloth and tall candles and gleaming silverware. It looked almost as pretty as last year's in Portland, though we had no autumn flowers. Just before we sat down to eat, he told us, "You're absolute wonders. I can't do any of those things you do and never could."

Being fair, Mama replied, "It was the Kimball family's helping us out that made all the difference. Remember, they used to work for us? They have been very nice to us, and they've lost their oldest son, too. Henry, I wrote you about that and about the girl from the sea, too."

"Yes, Nelline, of course, I recall those letters. I want to tell you that the Portland *Oregonian* reported that some Peninsula children had found an unknown young woman from an unreported shipwreck. It disappointed me that they didn't print your names, children, so I could boast about you. How is she?"

I told him, "Papa, we keep close watch on her through the Kimballs. Anna, who worked for us last summer, works at the Nahcotta Palace Hotel where the sick lady lives. She says the lady from the sea sleeps a lot. Sometimes, though, she wakes up and screams like she's having a bad dream, then goes back to sleep. She used to say 'mott,' but now she doesn't say anything at all. She just lies there in bed and stares through people with her golden eyes."

Papa exclaimed, "Golden, my word! Write me a special letter about how she's doing, Marcella."

I promised I would, and then I just sat silently during the grace which Papa said. He took a long, long time this year, being thankful about how nice our

Thanksgiving was in spite of our money troubles. I could see he was trying to tell us through the grace how proud he was of us and how sad he felt, and that hurt me.

After we'd all had a sample of the three different kinds of pies, we stayed at the table for a long while and talked. Papa told us about his business down in Portland, how painfully slow it was for him to get on his feet again. He'd sold our brick house and paid off the bank. He said how much he'd rather be living with us here at the beach than with his sister and brother-in-law as a guest. He also told us that he'd found a fine home for Dandy with a little girl who thought he was the best pony in Oregon, and that comforted us.

We all took Papa walking on the beach Saturday to show him exactly where we'd found the lady from the sea. He said he found the exercise bracing, and I could see that some color came back into his face.

How it hurt to say good-bye to him Sunday morning! We clung to him and hugged him, and Florence and I cried again. We went all the way to the steps of his railroad car for a farewell embrace.

It would be next year, 1896, at Eastertime, before we would see him again. He'd saved that bad news to tell us last.

When he took his valise from Alec and climbed up into the car, he looked down and said again, "I wish to God I could be here at Christmas with you, but I have to go see bankers in Chicago about a loan. I've got a business idea, but it's too soon to tell you about it. I hate to leave you, my dear ones."

Taking her handkerchief from her eyes, Mama told him, "Don't worry about us, Henry. We'll manage. We'll be fine. We'll send our Christmas presents to Portland in a few weeks so you'll have tokens of us before you go east."

I added bravely, "You bet we will. Take care of yourself, Papa. There's four of us here and only one of you wherever you go."

We stood beside the tracks waving as the train pulled out. Then we turned away, not wanting to look at it any longer. I was proud of Mama. I was proud of all of us Abbotts. I put my hand into hers as we walked home through the sand dunes and I said, "We're going to be all right at Christmas, aren't we?"

"Of course we are, Marcella. We got through Thanksgiving just fine, didn't we?"

"But Papa was here then!" wailed Florence.

"The five of us are still a family, dear," said Mama, "no matter where Papa happens to be. And that's what really counts."

Florence seemed comforted by that, and so was I.

It snowed a little the first week in December, but it didn't stay on the ground. Though flakes were falling when we walked to school, by the time we were on our way home there was only slush to wade through.

All the same, our feet got cold in our rubber boots.

We Abbotts were walking with Sarah and Evangeline, as we always did, when we saw Dr. Alf's old horse Rosinante coming toward us pulling the doctor's black buggy.

When he came abreast of us, he halted and asked, "Anybody here got the sniffles or wheezes or a cough or a rash?"

"Nosiree, Uncle Alf!" answered Sarah for all of us. His medicines did the job they were supposed to do, but they tasted terrible—"like sheep dip," Sarah had warned us. He kept big bottles of it in his buggy all the time.

To get his mind off his medicine, I asked, "How's the lady from the sea?"

"Sitting up and taking light nourishment. I'd say she was better."

Evangeline wanted to know, "When can we go visit her? After all, it was us who found her."

Sarah told her sister, "No, it was Marcy and me who did! So I should have been the one to ask him. All right, Dr. Alf, when *can* we come see her?"

"On next Saturday or Sunday, I'd say. But you won't be able to stay long. She's weak yet."

Alec asked, "Has she said who she is? Does she still say 'mott'?"

"No, I haven't heard her say that word anymore. She talks in her sleep, but no one can figure out what she's saying. It isn't English."

Not English? We stared at each other. I said, "Maybe she's French?"

"Maybe so."

Florence asked, "Does she talk Latin?"

"Definitely not. Nobody has spoken Latin except in church groups for well over a thousand years." He laughed. "I think we can rule Latin out."

Sarah asked, "Are you on your way to visit somebody sick?"

"No, not today. I'm exercising Rosinante for her arthritis, and I'm taking some fresh air for myself."

Evangeline came closer to the buggy and said one word. "Please!"

"Of course, I'm always glad to oblige a lady." He pulled out his pocket watch, opened it, and let her hear "The Blue Danube" all the way through to its end. We all held our breaths to catch its tinkle over the cries of the seagulls overhead.

When the waltz ended, Sarah asked, "Does the lady from the sea really have golden eyes?"

"You could call them that. They're yellow. I've never seen eyes like that before."

"Does she look straight at you, Dr. Perkins?" I asked.

"Yes, she looks at people now, but she doesn't try to make herself understood." He leaned over the buggy's side. "She's had a very rough time, what with being shipwrecked and cast adrift in the cold seas and breaking her leg and catching pneumonia. God knows how far out in the Pacific the ship went down or how many hours the poor girl floated. Her mind is affected by her suffering—and no wonder. The Lord knows how many people she lost in the wreck! Come along now, Rosinante; if we stand here much longer in this cold, your elbows will freeze. Good-bye, children."

And off they went while the Kimball girls laughed.

Alec looked at me and said, "I never heard of horses having elbows."

Evangeline told him, "They don't! Dr. Alf's only being funny to make us laugh. Do you want to go with us to see the washed-up lady Saturday morning? Pa's going to Nahcotta for supplies. We can all go there with him in our wagon."

"We'll ask our mother," came from Florence. "I think she'll say it's our duty to call on the poor sick lady. I just wish we had some flowers to bring her, but there aren't any in bloom. We always brought sick people flowers in Portland."

Sarah nodded. "We usually take them something to eat here. We'll bring her a jar of Ma's wild strawberry jam." Sarah was generous by nature. She added, "That jam could come from us Kimballs and you Abbotts, too."

I said, "Thank you, Sarah, but we'll bring something of our own. Mama knows how to make molasses taffy, you know, even though she isn't ready for jam-making yet. Mama's stuck at *G* in the cookbooks. That was for the Thanksgiving goose. *G* for goose came at the right time. Jams and jellies will come later on—after cake icing. That's under *I,* and we're sure looking forward to seven-minute boiled frosting. Our cakes under *C* have been sort of plain on top."

My friend Sarah nodded. "I bet your ma will be up to *J* by wild strawberry time in June, and maybe even beyond *J.*"

When the Kimballs' wagon showed up outside our house the next Saturday morning, Mama was ready to go, too. She had things to get in Nahcotta also. Mama climbed up to sit next to Mrs. Kimball on the seat, and off we went with all us kids in back.

As we rode off through the dunes, I asked, "Where's Miss Hester, Sarah?"

"Home—grading papers. She says she wonders why she ever decided to be a teacher. She says that teachers college in Oregon didn't tell her she'd have to grade papers over Saturday and Sunday. Hester works all the time."

Florence said, "Well, I guess teachers get summers off, too, to rest up."

Evangeline nodded. "Hester says by then she'll need to. We keep out of her way at home. We'll all look forward to a summer rest to sweeten her temper. Will you still be here then?"

"I don't know," I said. "That's up to Papa."

Sarah asked me, "Well, Marcy, what do you think of our beach life by now?"

I answered truthfully, "It's been exciting, even if there've been bad things, too." I looked into her dark-brown eyes. "But we've found out that Peninsula people can be real, true-blue friends if you give them a chance."

Evangeline asked, "Can't Portland folks be, too?"

"I think all the things we used to have down there, like our horses and pony and fancy house and clothes, got in the way of making real friends. Other kids were always counting up what we had and they didn't have." I laughed. "As soon as warm weather comes, I'm going barefoot. It looks like it feels good."

"It sure does," agreed Evangeline, who was looking down at her ugly black rubber boots, the kind we all wore.

Alec came in with, "I want summer to hurry up. I'm sick of rainwater going down the back of my neck from my sou'-wester hat when I bend backward."

Florence said, "I don't ever want to see or smell a bottle of fish oil again."

To change the subject, I said, "I wish we didn't have to leave Prince Albert home alone today." Red was in the wagon with us, curled up next to Evangeline, who was sheltering him from the rain with the bottom of her oilskin coat.

"You could have brought him," said Sarah. "There's room in here for another dog." Suddenly she looked straight at me and asked, "Did you make friends with us in the beginning only because Hester was going to be your teacher? Hester said you might, and I thought so, too, before she said so."

I felt my face getting red as the blood rose up into it. *Sarah knew!* I answered her as straight as she'd asked, "I guess that's true, Sarah. We were afraid not to act friendly because of her."

"Oh, rats!" said Evangeline. "Hester wouldn't treat you any different from anybody else here. She's fair."

I said, "We know that now, but we didn't then. Will you two forgive us?"

"Oh, sure." Sarah waved my question away with her hand like it had been silly. Then she added, "But I just had to ask you. I'm glad you told me the truth. We like you better because of that, don't we, Evangeline?"

"We sure do, Sarah."

I said, "Thank you for everything. If it wasn't for you, I don't know what we would have done here. You've been a big help to us and we admire you a lot."

Mama and Mr. and Mrs. Kimball went about their business in Nahcotta, while the five of us kids headed for our goal—the Palace Hotel and Eating House. We were ready and eager to see the shipwrecked lady like Dr. Alf said we could. He was out on a call, but Mrs. Rose Perkins was there. She met us at the front door, and beside her stood Anna Kimball in her maid's outfit.

Sarah told her aunt, "We came to see the washed-up lady. Dr. Alf said we could visit with her this morning."

"Yes, he warned me you'd be coming. Anna and I will take you up to her. Now, children, listen closely to what I tell you. Do not upset this young woman. Speak softly, and don't make any sudden movements. Don't touch her. You'll have only a few minutes with her, remember."

Anna offered, "She's awful weak yet."

Mrs. Perkins ordered, "Take off your oilskins and helmets and leave them on the front porch to drip. Wipe your boots on the welcome mat and go with Anna."

We did what Sarah and Evangeline's aunt told us to, and then we climbed up a flight of steps and went down a long hall behind Anna. Mrs. Perkins brought up the rear.

Anna opened a white-painted door, stuck her head in, and said, "There's some folks come to see you. These are the kids who found you on the beach when you got washed ashore. Maybe you'll remember them."

In we went, followed by Mrs. Perkins.

There in the big brass bed sat our lady from the sea. She was a little less pale than she'd been on the sand, or maybe it was the reflection from the rose-colored flannel gown she wore. Her eyes stared right at the five of us as we lined up at the foot of the bed. Florence had been right. Her eyes were golden.

Slowly the lady's hand came up to point at Florence, and she nodded her head. I gasped. She *remembered* my sister. Yes, she had opened her eyes at her on the beach that morning.

I whispered to Sarah, "She remembers it was Florence she looked at first of all!"

"Good," said Mrs. Perkins softly. "Speak to her, Florence, and then all you other children say something. Let her hear your voices. You were all there with her."

We said "hello" one after the other, but the lady didn't seem to take any notice of any of us except Florence. She stared and stared at her as we all looked at the lady.

Suddenly Florence asked, "Who are you? What's your name? My name is Florence," and she pointed to her chest.

There was a long silence. Then all at once the lady said, "Anna."

"Forevermore!" breathed Mrs. Perkins.

*"Anna!"* exploded Anna Kimball, pointing to herself.

But the lady from the sea shook her pale-golden head and touched her own breast. *"Anna!"* she said again.

*Her name!* We knew it now. Mrs. Perkins came quickly around to the side of the bed and sat down on the bright-colored quilt. She said to the lady, "Go on, dear. Your name is Anna. What is the rest of your name? Are you Anna Mott? What was the name of your ship?"

"Mott." The lady's eyes grew wild. "Mott!" Now she threw her white hands over her face, let out a wail, and started to sob.

# 9 WE GO TO ASTORIA

At Mrs. Perkins's orders, Anna Kimball ushered us quickly out of the room and shut the door. In the dark of the hallway she said, "It's winter now, so tourists don't come here to stay. Aunt Rose has the time to nurse the washed-up lady, but next summer she won't. She'll be too busy, and so will I. We have to find out about the lady before summer comes, or Dr. Alf will have to send her to Fort Steilacoom at the end of Puget Sound. That's the place where folks who are sick in the head live. Besides, she won't be able to stay here because she yells in the middle of the night like she's in the ocean again, and tourists staying here would leave because of her. They're mostly old folks with shaky nerves."

Now Anna grabbed Florence's hand and shook it. "Flossie, I don't know how you did it, but you busted through to her. It must be because she saw your face first of all. You did just fine."

My sister beamed with pride at the compliment.

After saying good-bye to Anna, we went out onto the front porch and put our foul-weather gear back on again. Then we went down into Nahcotta to find Mama and Mr. and Mrs. Kimball. They were having coffee and just-fried doughnuts in a cafe, and so we sat down with them. The place smelled like fish oil, naturally, because of the people in it, but the doughnuts tasted just fine.

Sarah and I took turns telling the grown-ups about the washed-up lady—how she had looked, what she'd done, and what she'd said.

When we were finished, Mr. Kimball said, "Well, well, this is interesting. I've got some ideas about her that might be worth discussing. It occurred to me that Anna is a common name. It's in the Bible, and a long time ago I knew a German girl by that name."

"Where?" asked Mrs. Kimball.

"Right here, when I was about ten years old. Since that poor shipwrecked lady is apparently not speaking English, maybe she'd be German."

Mama added, "Or Swedish or Danish or Norwegian or Dutch?"

Mrs. Kimball finished. "Or she could be Italian or Spanish or Portuguese. Does anybody know yet how she spells her name?"

I told her, "No. All she did was say it."

Sarah put in, "Why couldn't she be named something simple that's really American—like maybe Betsy, after Betsy Ross?"

Mr. Kimball nodded. "Sarah's right. The name Anna makes it hard to know exactly where she's from. I think Dr. Alf ought to take her down to Astoria as soon as she can travel and try her out on the foreigners down there. He might be able to round up folks who weren't born in America and speak other languages. There are generally more foreigners in port cities than in other places. Because of the amount of trade going on there with other countries, such folks are in demand. Dr. Alf'll know where to look. He knows lots of folks across the big river he can ask."

Mrs. Kimball said, "Perhaps he could take her there after Christmas. Her leg should be knitting well enough by then so she can use crutches to get around."

*Christmas!* Why did Mrs. Kimball have to say that sad word? I wasn't looking forward to it this year since we wouldn't see Papa. He'd already sent us a box of presents that we intended to open on Christmas Eve.

We'd sent him a box of presents, too. I'd knitted him a muffler. It was full of knots and holes, but full of love, too. Mama had made him a petit-point tobacco pouch for his pipe tobacco. Florence had made a red flannel pen wiper, and Alec had made a pipe holder for his pipes, carving out spaces for them. Last year we'd bought Papa a red velvet smoking jacket and a new meerschaum pipe.

I guess I must have let my sorrow show, because Sarah asked me, "What's wrong, Marcy?"

Florence answered for me. "We won't have Papa with us at Christmas."

"Oh!" Mrs. Kimball turned swiftly to Mama. "Why, Mrs. Abbott, you and your children must come share our Christmas with us!"

Mama said softly, "No, we couldn't intrude on your family holiday."

Mrs. Kimball went on, "It wouldn't be intruding. Our holiday will be more quiet than usual this year. We're going to miss our Whitney so." She touched Mama's hand. "We'd be very pleased to have you Abbotts with us. It will take our minds off other Christmases—ones we had with him."

I was proud of Mama as I heard her say, "Well, then, of course we'll come. How could we refuse? Thank you. Our gifts will be small, though."

Evangeline piped in, "Ours always have been. With eight of us kids, we never have a lot of money to spend on Christmas, but we have fun."

We Abbotts open presents on Christmas Eve, not Christmas morning. They were all under our Christmas tree, which Alec and Florence and I had cut down in the Peninsula woods and carried home. We had trimmed it with threaded popcorn and little bows of red and green calico left over from school dresses Mama had cut out and sewn for us. There were tiny candles all over it, stuck in tin holders Alec had made, and a tin-can star he'd cut for the very top. It wasn't one bit like our Portland tree of last year with its glass balls, English and German ornaments, and sparkling tinsel, but it was nice.

We opened Papa's box first and could see it was full of his love. He hadn't spent a lot of money, but it was clear he'd handpicked every gift. It wasn't like other years when he'd sent Mama or his secretary out with cash to buy things for all of us. He'd taken his own time off work to do it. It seemed to me that even if he wasn't here with us, his doing that himself brought us all closer to him than we'd been before.

Each of us got just one gift, wrapped in the same red paper. Mine was a brush-and-comb set and a mirror with mother-of-pearl in pretty patterns on the back. I'd use that every day for years and years to come and think of him while I brushed my hair. Florence received a box of watercolor paints and brushes from Germany, and Alec a dandy bone-handled pocketknife of English steel, because he liked to carve. Mama's present was surely different from last year's amethyst earrings. She received a book of French cooking with lots of recipes.

When we finished giving each other our presents, we sang carols. After we'd gone through "Adeste Fideles," Mama said, "I wonder if your father will be having Christmas dinner alone tomorrow in some dreary Chicago hotel."

I told her, "If he does, he'll be thinking of us with every bite he eats."

"Wishing he was here with us in Ocean Park," added Florence.

"Wishing he was eating Mama's cooking," came from Alec, who smacked his lips.

We all laughed at that. Mama had outdone herself on Christmas Eve dinner, giving us beefsteak and kidney pie because she had passed the letter *K* by now and was up to *O*. We also had oyster bisque made from Willapa Bay oysters and chess pie tarts. We'd never eaten better in Portland on December twenty-fourth.

We didn't dress up much to go to the Kimballs' to share their holiday, and we didn't bring Papa's gifts along to show them. We figured we were going to a strictly homemade Christmas.

As we walked over the dunes at noon in a drizzle, a sharp, chilly breeze off the ocean beat on our faces. Mama told us, "It will probably be a very simple Christmas, children, not like the one last year when we all went in our carriages from house to house visiting our friends and relations. The Kimballs are not rich, and they are in mourning."

Alec said, "We aren't rich either, Mama."

Mama smiled at him. "That's right. I sometimes wonder if we needed all that expensive fuss over holidays we used to make. I don't think we did. The first Christmas wasn't in a mansion, but in a manger. When you get older, I hope you will realize, as I have come to do, that the simpler things are often the deepest and the best. I think that's true of people, too. Do you miss Portland so very much now?"

I thought hard and finally said, "Not so much as I once did." The Palmer girls hadn't written me a Christmas letter—they'd just sent me a store-bought card. Florence had painted the one I sent them. Hers had been prettier in my estimation.

Florence told Mama, "I guess I don't miss it. All I really miss is Papa."

Alec had the last word, as usual. "All I miss outside of Papa is our pony. I wish we had a horse."

Mama told him firmly, "Alexander, you do not need a steed."

Florence giggled. "You made a poem, Mama."

"Well, so I did."

There was a wreath on the Kimballs' front door, not one of holly with red berries and a red ribbon, but a homemade evergreen one with a white bow on it. This sort of wreath showed there had been a death in the family.

All of the Kimballs were at home to greet us. Sarah took our wraps and Evangeline piled our little presents under the Christmas tree. Their tree looked a lot like ours, except that it had some glass ornaments.

Mr. Kimball made spiced wine for the grown-ups and gave us kids hot spiced cider. Pretty soon we all sat down to eat, and what a feast that was! We had oysters in their shells, a huge king salmon baked with lemony cream sauce, potatoes boiled in their jackets, cranberry muffins, and, for dessert, yellow and chocolate cakes piled high with fresh whipped cream. I didn't think any elegant cafe anywhere could touch it for goodness.

I heard Mama say, "Estella Kimball, you've got to tell me how you cooked that fish. Is that dill in the cream sauce?"

"Yes, it's there, Nelline. I grow it behind the woodshed. I'll tell you how I make it, of course."

Mama asked jokingly, "You won't leave out some ingredient to keep your secret, will you?"

"Never. Not to a friend."

After dinner we sang carols while Mrs. Kimball played the cottage organ. They were the same ones we had sung at home the night before.

Then one by one Mr. Kimball gave out the presents. We Abbotts gave all the Kimball females except Miss Hester pomander balls. These were oranges covered with whole cloves that had taken us hours to make. All of the males got blue satin sleeve garters Mama had sewn. In return, Florence and I got knitted red mittens and Alec a blue pair, and Mama received a purple crocheted shawl. What the Kimballs gave one another were all hand-crocheted or hand-knit, too, or carved or sewn.

Finally there wasn't anything left under the tree except for twelve little round packages all the same size, but wrapped in different colored papers.

Alec pointed and asked, "What're they?"

Mr. Kimball laughed. "I saved them till the last. They're all for Hester, it seems. Hasn't any one of you noticed Hester hasn't got one single gift yet?"

"I noticed," came from our teacher, who sat up very straight in her hard chair. Today she was dressed in dark garnet-red taffeta. She still wore her black armband.

Sarah, next to me on the settee, giggled and pinched me. We'd planned this the last time we'd gone to Ilwaco, and we'd brought Mr. Kimball into the joke. He brought Miss Hester her presents—one bright red shiny apple after another. She began to laugh when she opened the seventh one, and after she opened the last one, she said, "Should I make pies or cider?"

At that her father reached into the branches of the tree and brought out a bottle of lilac eau de cologne. He gave it to her, saying, "This isn't an ornament, though you are to us, Hester, dear. It's from your brothers and sisters for you to put on your hankies to keep out some of the fish-oil smells."

*　　*　　*

We went home after dark in the Kimball wagon. The rain had stopped and the sky was filled with stars that we could see between long, black streamers of clouds.

I told Florence and Alec, "It's been a good Christmas after all, though it would have been better with Papa here."

Alec said, "But then we wouldn't have got to go to the Kimballs' and see Miss Hester with twelve apples slipping around on her lap."

Florence told us all, "I bet we would have been asked there all the same—Papa, too. Isn't it quiet tonight, though?"

Almost as if he'd heard Florence's voice from the back, Mr. Kimball began singing "Silent Night," my favorite carol. He had a very good singing voice. We all chimed in with him.

On New Year's Eve and New Year's Day it rained and even snowed some. We stayed inside, playing games and reading books, while Mama sat in the kitchen figuring out what fancy dishes she could make from the ingredients available at Mr. Willard's store or in Nahcotta. Nobody came visiting that day. Just to get across the sand dunes they would have had to bend double against the wind. Thank heaven there weren't any shipwrecks!

We didn't visit the shipwrecked lady again or see

Dr. Perkins until the middle of January, when we met him coming back in his buggy from visiting a sick old man in Ocean Park.

Sarah flagged him down, grabbed Rosinante's bridle, and said, "How's the lady from the sea? Pa thinks you ought to take her to Astoria to see folks who don't speak English."

"Unhand my poor old horse, child. I plan to do that. The girl's physical health has improved enough for that, I'd say. She gets around on crutches now."

Sarah was surely bold. "Shouldn't Marcy and Flossie and Evangeline and Al and me come along with you? After all, we found her. It was Flossie who got her to tell us her name."

Dr. Perkins frowned. "Well, I don't know about that. Five's a lot of kids for me to ride herd on."

Sarah promised, "We won't be a bit of trouble—honest."

I added, "We could help you with the lady. I talk some French."

He shook his head. "We tried her on that—read from a book. We showed her the book, too, but no luck. I read her some medical-school German books I used to read, but she only looked at us and blinked. Maybe it's the way I pronounce things, but she didn't respond. I tried her on a bit of Latin, too, and for a minute I got a flash of something from her."

"What?" cried Florence.

"I said 'mater,' which is Latin for 'mother,' and pretended like I was carrying a baby in my arms. She watched me, nodded, and said 'mott' again. I think 'mott' might mean 'mother' in her language, but I don't know which one she's speaking. I believe she wants her mother. After what happened to her, who wouldn't?"

I said softly, "I wonder if her mother could have been on that ship?"

"Perhaps. I thought then of her father, so I pointed to my beard and said 'pater,' which is Latin for 'father,' than 'pere' in French and 'vater' in German. None of them worked at all. She said something odd like 'oh-tets' and pointed to me, and that was that."

" 'Oh-tets'?" muttered Alec as we all stared at one another.

Dr. Alf interrupted our staring. He told us, "All right, you five be at the train depot at nine sharp the first Saturday in February if you want to go to Astoria with me. Don't bring lunches. This will not be any picnic."

"What will we eat?" asked Evangeline for all of us.

"You let me worry about that." Then he asked us, "What about wheezes, sneezes, swollen glands, sore throats, pinkeye, rashes, or boils? Everybody stick out your tongues."

We did. He leaned out to inspect us, grunted, and said, "Healthy and pink as I've ever seen. I don't want the lady I saved from pneumonia to come down with your chicken pox or mumps or measles or scarlatina.

Keep well. If you get sick, keep away from the depot the first Saturday in February. Giddap, Rosinante. My hot coffee's waiting at the hotel."

As Dr. Alf drove away, Sarah turned to the rest of us with a wide smile on her face. She said wonderingly, "Golly, he said we could come—*all of us!* He never asked us to Astoria before."

Since we would be going with Dr. Perkins, Mama gave her permission for us to go to Astoria. We could hardly wait through the rest of January. To keep ourselves well, we were careful not to get our feet wet and to steer clear of kids with head colds.

By eight-thirty the morning of the fourth of February, we were at the depot in our boots and oilskins, but underneath those we had on our best clothes.

The Kimball sisters soon met us there in the waiting room and, a few minutes before nine, Dr. Alf showed up with Ced Perkins in the hotel wagon. The pale lady was with him, wearing Mrs. Perkins's warm navy-blue coat and a wool plaid shawl over her head and shoulders. The blue-green-and-black plaid made her look paler than ever.

When the train came, Dr. Alf helped her get aboard with her crutches, and the five of us followed. We sat quiet as mice to please Dr. Alf while the train began its southward journey to Ilwaco. At first the lady from the sea grabbed at him as it jerked away from the station, crying out and looking wild-eyed. Dr. Alf patted her hand, and she finally let go and leaned back to look out the train windows at gray Willapa Bay on our left.

Sarah whispered to me, "She's never been on a train before or she'd know how they jerk to start out. She got scared."

I whispered back, "Did you see how she stared at the train when she arrived at the depot? I don't think she ever saw a train till now. But there are trains everywhere in the world nowadays. Where could she come from where there aren't any?"

"I don't know, Marcy," Sarah replied, then asked Dr. Alf, "Where are we going to in Astoria?"

"First the hospital, and then, if we must, to every eating house there that isn't owned by an English-speaking person. Which is why you didn't have to bring your lunches. We will have to eat wherever we go."

"Golly!" exclaimed Alec and Florence. They just loved to eat in restaurants.

To get to Astoria from Ilwaco, we had to take a ferry over the Columbia River. I watched the lady from the sea now, too, and saw how she clung to Dr. Perkins and hung back, not wanting to go aboard. Yes, she seemed afraid of the water, and who could blame her?

Astoria wasn't as big as Portland, but it was much bigger than Nahcotta. It had salmon canneries that were built on docks stretching out into the river, while the town itself spread out behind the docks and climbed up the cliffs that backed it.

When we got off the ferry, we walked through the streets and up a steep hill to the hospital. Dr. Alf had to help the lady from the sea as we went along. Once we arrived at the hospital, we sat on a bench in a long hall that smelled of medicine while Dr. Alf disappeared through a door with her.

While we were sitting in the hallway, we didn't see anything but nurses in long white dresses and little white caps going up and down. Nor did we hear anything but the swishing of their clothes. Alec found out that by leaning our heads against the back wall and pressing our ears to it we could hear voices— Dr. Alf's and some other man's. But the voices were too muffled for us to make out anything they were saying.

Finally, Dr. Perkins, the lady from the sea, and a short, heavyset bald man came out into the hall. The bald man was saying in a deep voice, "I'm a Finn, but I speak Swedish and can understand Norwegian, as well as Danish when the Danes don't gurgle at me. I have spoken to this young woman in all four languages and am convinced that she didn't understand a word I said. I have no idea what nationality she is. You say you've tried French and German?"

"Yes, Dr. Kallinen," said Dr. Alf. "These children here found her on the beach." He nodded toward us. "The girl spoke her name to one of them. She said

'Anna.' She will turn her head toward people who say it."

"Wait a minute." Dr. Kallinen walked away and came right back with a black-covered book I knew was the Bible. He thumbed to the New Testament, hunted a bit, and said, "Anna was the name of the mother of Mary. Here it is in print, right where my fingernail is. This young woman may have trouble with speech, but perhaps she can read. Bring her here, please."

When Dr. Alf took the lady from the sea over to the book, Dr. Kallinen tapped the verse where the name was. He said loudly, "This is the name 'Anna' right here. See?"

We watched the pale lady look at the page. She looked at Dr. Alf, then at us, and shook her head. She didn't recognize her own name! Maybe she couldn't read at all. She gently took the Bible from the Finnish doctor, closed it, and handed it back to him, still shaking her pale golden head.

Dr. Alf sighed. He asked, "Dr. Kallinen, one more question. Would you know some of the foreign-food restaurants and any people who speak languages other than those you and I have tried on her?"

Dr. Kallinen pursed his lips, then said, "There aren't too many such cafes here. There's a Greek one and an Italian and a Portuguese. They're all on Bond Street. That'd be it, so far as I know."

"Thank you for all of your help," Dr. Alf said as he shook the other man's hand. Turning to us, he ordered, "Now we head for Bond Street and lunch."

And so we did. We started up one side of the street, stopping at the Greek restaurant. As we ate big slices of cheese pie with black olives and spinach inside, Dr. Alf spoke to the owner, a big man with curling gray hair and a black mustache, and asked him to speak Greek to the lady from the sea. The man did, but she only stared at him and looked sad.

Next we went to the Italian cafe, where the lady cook spoke Italian to her. But our lady only shook her head and looked sadder. We had plates of spaghetti and meatballs there, and because the cook felt so sorry for the lady from the sea, we also ate big dishes of spumoni ice cream on the house.

After that, we went to the Portuguese cafe where a very handsome dark-eyed man, the owner's son, spoke Portuguese, then Spanish, to her. He even sang a sad song for her, playing a mandolin. Once more our lady shook her head as tears came to her eyes. She seemed to know what Dr. Alf was trying to do for her. Of course, we had to eat there, too, and we did—some spicy, yellow-colored fish stew that Dr. Alf said had saffron in it.

Once we were back out on Bond Street again, I felt so stuffed I could hardly walk. The salty cheese and garlicky spaghetti and saffron in the stew were fighting a war in my stomach.

I stood on the sidewalk and looked at Dr. Alf, who was loosening his collar and unbuttoning his waistcoat. Florence and Alec had gone sort of gray in the face, while the Kimballs had gone reddish. The lady from the sea was her usual self. She'd scarcely eaten a bite anywhere we'd been.

Sarah gulped out, "Well, we sure didn't learn anything except how foreign folks cook, did we?"

"Not a blessed thing," said the doctor. He spoke to the lady. "Unless you come from the Balkans, my dear, you must come from the moon or Mars."

In spite of the pain in my midsection, I had an idea. I asked, "Dr. Perkins, did you ever try her on a map?"

His bulging eyes brightened. "That's a capital idea, Marcella. I didn't have an atlas back at the Palace Hotel. We'll try her on maps in the bookstore across the street. Perhaps she did come from the Balkans, after all—or from Turkey or some place in the Near East."

So we all waddled our way across the street, between buggies and wagons, and then the five of us stood waiting while Dr. Alf asked to see an atlas.

The little lady clerk staggered out of a back room with a huge book and banged it down on the counter. Dr. Alf led the lady from the sea to it and opened the book to the map of Europe. We watched him touch the countries on two big pages with his finger, naming them one by one—starting with Ireland and traveling east into Asia. She leaned on her crutches watching him, looking interested, but she only shook her head at each one he touched.

Once again he sighed, then thanked the clerk, bought a pocket dictionary to repay her for her help, and led us all outside. He told us, "We're going back home now, but we are somewhat wiser than we were before we came. I've concluded that she does come from the moon. I'd hoped to find her own people for her."

I tugged at his sleeve, which was a bold thing to do because I wasn't related to him. "Does that mean she's going to have to go to the place where people who aren't right in the head go to live?" I didn't want to use the words "crazy" or "mad" or "insane" for our lady.

"I am afraid so, child. The doctors there are trained to deal with mental troubles. They will know more than I do about such matters. Perhaps the shock of being in the ocean or her high fever affected her mind permanently so that nothing we try will ever rouse her. Come on to the ferry now. Walking downhill should shake down some of that food we ate."

At the ferry landing, Dr. Perkins turned around to tell us five unhappy children, "You may become queasy on the ferry after all you've eaten. If you need to get sick, be sure to run to the side of the boat where the wind is at your back, not at your front."

"Oh, I won't get sick!" boasted Alec.

He did, though, five minutes after the ferry pulled away from the dock. As we rocked up and down in the choppy Columbia River, he was the first to run for the rail. Florence was next, and then me, holding my poor stomach with both hands. The two Kimballs held out longer.

When our aching insides were all cleaned out, Sarah came over to whisper to me, "Look at Dr. Alf. He's green and sweating. I bet you a dime he can't last till we dock in Ilwaco."

I didn't take her bet. By looking at him I could tell I would lose my dime. Just before the ferry docked, he went to the rail, carefully took out his upper and lower false teeth, put them into his coat pockets, leaned over, and lost his three lunches, too.

The lady from the sea was the only one of us who didn't get sick. Throughout the ferry ride, she just stood holding onto the rail and looked down at the dark gray river or stared out to its mouth, where so many ships had foundered in the past.

How I wished we could help her!

# 10

# AN ACT OF GOD

Spring arrived and so did Papa, looking pale compared to us beach people. He came to be with us over Easter. Mama made a roast ham dinner and spice cake with boiled seven-minute icing for dessert. By now she'd gone through the cookbooks we had all the way through *V*, though she didn't really bother anymore to go by the alphabet only. After all, once she reached veal there wasn't much else.

Papa told her she looked even finer than last November and had roses in her cheeks and stars in her eyes. She told him, "Henry, that's because I hang up our own laundry out on our own lines in the wind and sunshine. I walk on the dunes a lot. I get exercise and fresh air. Most of all, I think I feel healthier because I feel useful here. I like feeling useful."

"Well, being useful surely brings out a bloom in you, Nelline. You look like a girl again." He told Florence and me, "By summer you girls will be just bursting with health, as the poets say. That goes for you, too, Alec. You're some inches taller. I had worried about you. But I think you look splendid and you are doing splendidly, even better than when I was here last. I very much enjoyed your letters about your Christmas here and about the events since then."

Alec told him, "We bought seeds in Nahcotta and planted a vegetable garden. It's coming up fine. I weed it and work on it all the time."

"That's very good to hear. I'll be sure to go out and admire it before I leave for Portland tomorrow." Then he paused and said, "I'm working on a surprise for all of us."

I cried out first, "What is it?"

"If I told you, Marcella, it wouldn't be a surprise, would it?"

Florence wheedled, "Then, when will we find out?"

"This summer. Surprises sometimes take time. It wasn't easy to pull off. It took a lot of letters and bargaining. I hope it all will go through the way I want it to. Things have been tricky for me lately. I mean tricky in business details you wouldn't understand until you're older. I won't even tell your mother. She would understand, but I don't want to worry her."

Worry? More worries? Wouldn't they ever end?

Before I could ask Papa about this, Alec burst out with, "Has the surprise got anything to do with you going to Chicago?"

Papa lifted his hands. "No more about this now. No more coaxing me. Tell me about that woman who came ashore tied to the mast."

I said, "Papa, I wrote you all about our trip to Astoria with the doctor and her in February."

"Yes, but that was weeks ago. How is she now? You haven't written about her lately."

I looked to my sister and brother and said, "I'm the oldest, so I'll talk first, all right?"

"I guess so," said Florence, who hadn't liked hearing that.

"All right," said Alec, who wanted to impress Papa, too.

I planted my elbows comfortably on the table and started in. "We've been to visit her just about every Saturday since then. She's up more, and now she's walking around the Palace Hotel with her crutches. She's even helping out Mrs. Perkins, washing dishes and doing things like that. She can stir laundry while it boils and clean a stovetop, but she can't use an iron. She sort of earns her keep there, but they can't have her any more once the tourists start to come. She still has nightmares and screams in her sleep. Sometimes she just sits and stares at the wall. Mrs. Perkins says it's nerve-wracking."

Papa asked, "Did anybody ever find out anything about the ship she was on?"

"Not a thing. Dr. Alf and Ced Perkins kept checking and the Lifesaving Service did, too. They sent telegrams all up and down the coast and to Mexico and Canada and Alaska, but there doesn't seem to be any ship reported missing anywhere."

"Most unusual, Marcella. Does the girl speak now?"

Florence burst in with, "Sort of, but what she says is kind of wild. You can't trade a word in English with her for one in whatever language it is she speaks. I showed her a plate at the hotel and said 'plate,' and she pointed to her dress and said 'platya.' She gets things muddled up in her head."

"You bet," agreed Alec. "We took Prince Albert to see her, and she looked at him like she couldn't believe that's what a dog looks like. She sure never saw an English bulldog before."

I said, "She's seen cats, though. She calls the hotel mouser 'cot'—it sounds like she's talking about a bed."

Florence added, "She drinks tea, but only from a glass, not a cup. The first time Mrs. Perkins tried to give her some coffee, the lady ran to the back door and spit it out. She uses spoons for vegetables and things like that, but she drinks soup out of her bowl. Dr. Alf won't let her have a knife of any kind. He's afraid she might hurt herself with it. Sometimes all at once she starts to cry, and she cries and cries and tears at her hair with her hands. Other times she's all right. But she never smiles."

"Well, children, I can understand why she doesn't. But it appears to me Dr. Perkins has left no stone unturned for her welfare."

"He sure hasn't," I agreed.

Papa turned to Mama to ask, "Nelline, have you seen this unfortunate girl?"

"Just once. She was in a Nahcotta store with Mrs. Perkins. She had the saddest expression I think I've ever seen. She's a stranger in a world that is completely foreign to her. Mrs. Perkins told me she didn't even know what a corset or a curling iron was. Evidently she has never tasted chocolate or an orange or white bread, and she didn't know what the kitchen pump or the parlor piano were. Miss Hester Kimball, the teacher, went to the hotel to play some old American and English songs for her on the hotel piano, but they didn't seem to be anything the girl had ever heard. Miss Kimball played every foreign tune in her music books, too, but nothing happened."

Alec piped up, "Dr. Alf says the ship she was on must have fallen straight down to the bottom of the ocean from the moon."

Florence said dreamily, "With her pale skin and golden eyes, she's sort of like a lost maiden from the moon."

Alec laughed at her and made us all laugh when he said, "Not the way she eats cabbage and corned beef at the hotel, she isn't any moon lady. She sure likes cabbage."

By the time May came and brought warm weather with it, we Abbotts were running around bareheaded and barefoot nine-tenths of the time, just like the Kimball sisters and Joel, the champion chicken-plucker. But even though we found out we didn't sunburn didn't mean that we'd forgotten Prince Albert's nose did. We always took him out with his umbrella, and in our hearts we knew he was grateful. He was that kind of dog. Though we'd all lived at the beach for months now, there was still something Port-landish about him. Maybe it was because he was so slow and stately while Red, the Kimball dog, ran in yapping circles around him, darting into the surf to bite waves. Prince Albert just sat on the sand while we dug clams and raked for crabs in crab holes in the sand with the Kimballs and Joel.

All of us did just fine in school, judging from the grades Miss Hester gave us—honest grades. Like Sarah had told me, she was fair. Nobody was ever her pet.

One afternoon as we all walked home together after school, I asked Sarah, "Doesn't Miss Hester have a beau?"

Sarah laughed. "There's a surfman at the Klipsan Beach Lifesaving Service Station that has his eye on her, I think. He used to dance with her a lot when she and Whit went to the dances at the lodge in Ilwaco. Hester says she won't go to dances now for a year out of respect to Whit."

I nodded. Yes, she still wore a black crepe band on her arm. I asked, "Is she sweet on the surfman?"

Evangeline answered, "We don't know. Last summer Anna once asked her at supper, just to tease her. She told us to mind our own business, if we please. She doesn't ever forget she's a schoolteacher now." She frowned. "You know, she made herself a new dress last year. It's real pretty—peach-colored taffeta with a Jersey-cream-colored lace bertha and leg-of-mutton sleeves and pearl buttons all up the back. She had it on only once, when she'd just finished making it. We thought she'd wear it at Easter, but she didn't. She could have worn the black band with it and folks would have understood. That's strange, I think."

"Why?" asked Alec.

"Because Ma says ladies want to show off something that's new and pretty and wear it somewhere right away. Hester loaned some of her nicest clothes to the washed-up lady."

Florence asked, "She'll get them back when the pale lady has to go away, won't she?"

Sarah answered, "Yes, she won't need Hester's things where she's going. Dr. Alf says patients there wear special clothes—bathrobes and wrappers and gowns and things like that."

I said, "It sounds like she's going to a kind of prison, huh?"

Sarah sighed. "That's what Ma and Pa say, too. But nobody here on the Peninsula can take care of her the way she is. Could you folks do it?"

Now I sighed. "We haven't got the money for any more than the four of us and our dog. That's why we're up here, remember?"

"And we're glad you are, but not for that reason," said my friend as she put her arm around my waist.

I said, "Thank you, Sarah Kimball!"

According to the Kimballs, the last part of May was the right time to go looking for patches of the little fingernail-sized wild strawberries that out-tasted any you could buy in a market or grow in a garden. Sarah said we could even smell our way to them if we closed our eyes and followed their talcum-powder perfume over the sand dunes. We were going to go wild strawberry stalking with Sarah and Evangeline early on a Saturday morning, so we got up before Mama did and I made breakfast. I cooked pancakes on the Old Dickens, making some extra ones so we could take them to the dunes with us, rolled up with Mrs. Kimball's raspberry jam inside them like crepes from one of Portland's French cafes.

But we didn't get through breakfast at all that morning. We'd just about sat down when we heard the noise of hoofbeats. It was Prince and Maude, with the Kimball girls riding them bareback.

I flung open our kitchen window, stuck my head out, and shouted, "What's the matter? It isn't seven yet. We haven't had our pancakes."

Sarah called back to me, "Grab them off the plate and climb aboard. A neighbor just told Pa that something else has washed up on the ocean beach."

"What is it? Another lady?" yelped Florence beside me at the window. "There wasn't a storm again last night."

"It isn't a person. It's something else," shouted Evangeline.

I let out my breath. Thank heavens, it wasn't a drowned sailor.

"Well, what is it?" demanded Alec, shoving his head under Florence's and my chins.

"It's a whale!"

"A *whale?*" squealed my brother so loudly it hurt my ears.

Sarah waited until Prince had turned an excited circle from all our yelling. Now she shouted, "It's a great big one, the neighbor says."

"It's supposed to be a whale of a dead whale!" sang out Evangeline. "Hurry up. Come on out."

We didn't wait to shut the window. While I wrote a note to Mama telling her where we had gone, Florence and Alec put the pancakes into napkins and ran

out the back door. They were already up on one of
the big white horses when I got there. I took hold of
the strong hand Sarah offered me and swung up behind her.

A whale. A whale right here in Ocean Park! I'd
never seen one before.

As we cantered west to the sea, I asked Sarah, "Has
a whale ever come ashore here before?"

"Not for a long, long time. Come on, Prince, go as
fast as you can. Hang on tight, Marcy. Let's see if he
can get up a gallop on the plank road."

Well, it truly was a whale of a whale, the biggest
thing I'd ever seen. It lay on the sand where the high
tide had left it early that morning. It was so large that
it blotted out the ocean behind it. It was on its belly,
its huge head flat as if it lay on its chin, with its fan-
shaped tail and fins spread out to its sides and rear.
I guess you could say it was sprawled out—sprawled
out and, for sure, as dead as could be. One look at it
would show anybody with eyes the whale wasn't
breathing. You couldn't miss seeing something that
size breathing. I didn't know much about whales, but
I did know that they weren't fish and that they
breathed air just like we did.

Our first sight of the whale stopped cold any talk
among us. Sarah and Evangeline halted the big horses
at the top of the last dune before the wet beach sand
began.

Alec was the first to say anything. "Golly, it's big as a house!"

"Bigger than some sheds here on the Peninsula," agreed Evangeline.

I asked, "Should we go down to it, Sarah?"

"I don't see why not, Marcy. Some folks are there already. I can see Dr. Alf's buggy and Rosinante down there, can't you?"

By squinting I could just make them out beside the dark carcass of the whale. There were other buggies and some wagons on the beach, too. We wouldn't be the first.

"Come on, Evangeline," ordered Sarah, and Prince and Maude started slowly down the slope as yellow sand slipped under their large hooves. It was dangerous to move fast going uphill or downhill in dry sand.

We walked the horses through the driftwood and kelp tangles until we got to hard sand. Then we let them canter.

Up close the whale was even bigger. When we had first seen it, it had looked black, but up close we could see it was dark gray with some lighter gray in spots. It had a gigantic head with hairs on it, while the rest of it was covered with barnacles.

I'd read the word "awe" in books, but until now I hadn't known what it really meant. The feeling that went with that word took any other words right out of my mouth. None of us said a thing. We just sat on our horses and stared.

Then I heard Dr. Perkins say, "A true leviathan of the deep! That is what this is."

Another man told him, "Alf, I know what kind of whale this one is. I served on a whaling ship when I was a boy. This here ain't no everyday gray whale you see in herds passing up and down the coast every January or February on their way to warm-water mating grounds in Mexico. This is a humpback whale. They ain't so common."

I found my voice to ask, "What did it die of, mister?"

A yellow-bearded man I'd seen in Nahcotta at the general store told me, "Lord only knows, little girl. What can kill anything this big? Maybe it just got old and tired and knew its time was up, so it died and floated to shore as a present to us."

Dr. Alf had been walking around the whale and now told everyone, "I was here very early because I'd been up all night to deliver a baby nearby, a fine baby girl. I came home along the beach for some air and exercise for Rosinante. This animal's been harpooned in the past by whale hunters, but the wounds have healed and there aren't any fresh ones. Sharks and killer whales haven't been harrying it." He sighed. "The sea has been all too generous to us with its gifts lately, hasn't it? First that poor shipwrecked girl and now this whale, and both of them are problems."

"You're right, Alf," agreed the yellow-bearded man. "You're stuck with the first one and we're all stuck with this second one. What'll we do with this whale? We can't wait around too long to make up our minds. Warm weather's coming and it won't be long before it starts to smell. Once when I was a boy, a little pilot whale come ashore here, and we buried it. But this one'll take a real big hole. That's going to take a long time to dig with our shovels."

I said, "Can't you put ropes around it and pull it to the water with horses? Then once it's afloat you can tow it out to deep water."

The yellow-bearded man looked at me. "This is a smart little girl. We already talked about that. But we figured that the next tide would just bring it back onto the sand."

Sarah told him, "I got a good idea. Do what Marcy says and tow it down below the Columbia River to Oregon. Then the tide will bring it ashore down there."

Another man laughed. "There's one thing about a whale, kid. You can't hide where it first came ashore. Whale news travels fast. The telegraph-office people in Nahcotta are probably sending the news off to Portland and Seattle right this very minute. They've been here already. Oregon folk will know it's a Peninsula whale we're giving them and will tow it back here. They may even take us to court over dumping our nuisance on them."

Evangeline asked, "Can't you tow it out and fill its mouth with rocks and sink it?"

Dr. Alf smiled up at her. "It would take tons of rocks. And we don't have any on this beach. And how would we get its mouth open when it's so huge? Jake here has suggested we use dynamite on it, but I say no. The explosion would litter Ocean Park and Nahcotta with pieces of rotting flesh. That would bring flies and maybe sickness, and we'd still have the smell."

Sarah asked, "What can we do, then?"

"Not a blessed thing, child. Let nature take her course and leave the whale to decompose."

A Nahcotta man who'd just ridden up on a gray horse laughed harshly. "That could take all summer, Doc. Nobody will want to come to the beach because of the smell. And any seawater that touches the whale is going to turn foul. It'll be hell living here while nature takes her course. I run a business in Nahcotta only a mile away from here. Some of you know my livery stable. Well, I rent horses and buggies to tourists, and summer's when I make all my money. Tourists will show up, take one whiff of this, and go down to Oregon. They'll find some clean beach someplace else."

Dr. Perkins nodded. "What you say is true. What we need is a blessed miracle, like a nice big tidal wave, to come along and take our problem away with it. But then it could also take our houses and us and part of the Peninsula away with it, too. The way I see it, this whale will have to be endured all summer."

He turned to the Kimballs and us Abbotts. "Tell your mothers to have well-boiled sheeting ready to make masks out of. Pretty soon you're going to have to wear them over your noses and mouths. Everybody will. We'd also better lay in a supply of perfume to put on the masks. We'll be needing that. And pray for cool weather—the cooler the better!"

# 11
# A BLESSED MIRACLE

When we got home, Sarah and Evangeline let their horses graze in the long grass growing on one side of our house while we all ran inside to tell Mama the news.

Alec yelled out as he jerked the back door open, "Hey, Mama, we've been to the ocean and there's big news on the beach!"

Mama, who was just peeking into the oven door of the Old Dickens, said, "Yes, I read Marcella's note about the whale."

Florence cried, "It's bigger than anything I've ever seen before."

I cried next, "It's not alive. Dr. Perkins said we'd better pray for cool weather to last as long as it can."

"Oh, dear." Mama sat down. "I can't think of anything we need less than a dead whale. What will the Peninsula men do?"

Sarah spoke now. "They don't know what to do. It's the biggest whale that's ever come ashore—too big to bury. It'd take every man and shovel from Ilwaco to Oysterville to do it. Dr. Alf says nature will have to take her course."

Mama shuddered. "Nobody'll have much of an appetite after that course of nature has started. Maybe we'd better pray for hot weather, to get it over faster. Stay here, all of you. We'd best eat while we can enjoy it. I'm making my very first puff pastry right now."

"What's that?" asked Evangeline.

"Fancy French cooking," I told her. My, but Mama was coming along splendidly in the cookbooks! She was getting bolder and bolder and must have gone back to *E* and eclairs. Puff pastry was hard to cook. You only got it in French cafes in Portland.

She said, "Forget the whale for a while. I've got cream to whip once the puff shells have come out and dried a bit."

Evangeline said, "Ma whips cream to put on top of our birthday cakes, but I've never seen it put in a puffy shell."

"Well, you will now. A proper piece of puff pastry will melt in your mouth. I'll put powdered sugar on them to top them off."

An hour later we had golden pastries three inches high filled with white whipped cream and dusted with sugar. They were wonderful!

"My golly," came from Sarah as she finished hers. "You're turning into a better cook than Ma. Can you cook all the things we get from the sea and bay around here?"

Mama laughed. "Oh, yes. Crab cakes and oyster stew and fried oysters and clam chowder and fried clams and any fish that swims hereabouts."

Alec said, "We eat just fine."

Evangeline had powdered sugar on her nose. She came out with, "You ought to start a bakery somewhere, Missus Abbott, and make nothing but cream puff shells."

"Why, thank you, Evangeline. I never thought I'd take so well to cookery."

"She means it, ma'am," agreed Sarah. "Folks'd pay to buy these."

"But isn't there a French bakery in Astoria?" Mama asked.

Sarah and Evangeline both shook their heads. "We never heard of any," came from Sarah. "If there was, Dr. Alf would have taken the washed-up lady to it to hear real French, not the kind he read from a book."

"Yes, of course." Mama's face sobered. "That poor girl. She'll have to leave soon, won't she?"

"Yes'm. Aunt Rose Perkins says she'll travel to Fort Steilacoom with her when she goes," Sarah told her.

Evangeline nodded. "Bad as it may be for her to leave here, at least she won't have to smell our whale. Dr. Alf said you and Ma better start thinking of masks for us to wear and something sweet-smelling to put on them. Ma doesn't use perfume, but she keeps lots of vanilla on hand."

"So do I," said Mama. "Vanilla and lemon extract are much cheaper than perfumes, and more practical, too."

Sarah laughed. "Ma says more men are caught as husbands by the good smells coming out of a kitchen than out of perfume bottles."

The rest of that day and the next one were cloudy and cool, so we got a little bit of a reply to our prayers while all of us Peninsula people tried to figure out what to do about our whale.

Because of it, Miss Hester gave us a whole day of lessons about whales. After school that afternoon, we went with the Kimballs to the Palace Hotel with a message from Mrs. Kimball to her sister. We saw Dr. Alf and Rosinante at the railroad depot. He was sitting in his rig like he was waiting for somebody to come in on the Ilwaco train, which was due any minute.

We all went up to him, and listened to his musical watch, and then Sarah asked, "Who're you waiting for?"

"Christmas, Sarah."

"Christmas was a long time back. Who are you really waiting for?"

"A certain Dr. Peter Blessed, who sent me a telegram from San Francisco three days ago."

Evangeline asked, "What did it say?"

"I should say 'none of your beeswax' but, because you are so insistent, all right." He reached into his vest pocket and pulled out a piece of yellow paper, which he handed to Evangeline. "Here, read it out loud, Evvie."

Evangeline read it. " 'I read about your problem in the San Francisco newspaper. Coming to consult with you about it. Expect me on the four o'clock train from Ilwaco, May twenty-third. Dr. Peter Blessed.' "

"Dr. Blessed?" asked Sarah. "Who's he?"

Dr. Alf laughed. "Blessed if I know, dear. He must have read about my problems with the lady from the sea. She's quite a dilemma."

"What's a dilemma?" asked Alec.

"A big mess you don't know what to do anything about, my lad."

I said, "Like the whale on the beach?"

"Yes, that's a dilemma, too."

At that very moment, Miss Hester came up to us

with a portfolio of our school papers to grade. She must have followed us through the high dunes, where we didn't see her.

She asked, "Dr. Alf, are you expecting somebody on the train today?"

"Yes, a Dr. Blessed from San Francisco said he's coming." And he showed her the telegram, too.

After she read it, she said, "He must be a doctor who specializes in the brain. Perhaps he can help you with your patient."

"Maybe so, Hester, but I don't know him by name from Adam's off-ox. Children, that is the ox nobody in the world knows the name of, so do not ask me. This man coming is a perfect stranger to me, but I trust he is a medical man who deals with mental illness."

I said, "Whoever he is, he's come a long way to talk to you. It isn't easy getting here. I wonder how he heard about the lady from the sea being sick way down in San Francisco."

"I don't know, Marcella. Perhaps the papers there have written an article about her lately. He would have had to come all the way up through northern California and Oregon, then west to Astoria on the railroads and over the Columbia on the ferry, and then up to here. He ought to be exhausted if he's done all that in three days."

Sarah said, "I never saw a head doctor before."

Florence put in, "Let's hang around and get a gander at him. I bet he's old and has a long gray beard."

I added, "And silver-rimmed eyeglasses."

"And a checkered suit," came from Alec.

"And shiny, polished, black leather boots," said Sarah.

Nothing would have got us away from the depot—nothing at all, not even an order from Miss Hester or Dr. Alf, who didn't give any. And Miss Hester stayed right with us.

Were we ever wrong about Dr. Blessed! He didn't wear glasses or a checkered suit. He had on a brown suit and brown shoes, not boots at all. His hair was red under his brown derby hat, and his face was freckly but handsome. He wasn't anywhere so old as Dr. Alf or Papa, but somewhere between Miss Hester's age and Mama's.

How did we know who he was? That was easy. We knew everybody else who got off the train because they were all Nahcotta people.

Dr. Blessed stood looking around, beside his valise and a carpetbag, until Dr. Alf got out of the buggy and walked over to him. Of course, we went up right behind Dr. Alf, and so did Miss Hester.

We heard our doctor say, "Dr. Blessed, I presume?"

"Yes, sir, that's me," said the other doctor, and they shook hands.

Dr. Perkins said, "I'll take you over to the Palace Hotel. That's where you'll be seeing our problem—as you put it in your telegram."

"*Hotel?*" Dr. Blessed looked surprised. "In a *house*, sir?"

"Yes, we couldn't leave her on the beach where we found her washed up, could we?"

"You *moved* her?"

"Of course. It was the honorable thing to do."

Dr. Blessed was staring very oddly at Dr. Alf. Now he asked, "You are certain it is a she, not a he?"

Dr. Alf was staring very oddly at Dr. Blessed by now. He said, "Of course I'm sure. I am a medical doctor, you know. She's getting the best care I can give her, and lots of fresh ocean air."

"Yes, of course. Air is vital to all *living* things. The newspaper article I read must have been in error. You see, I came here hoping to dispose of the specimen for you."

"She's no specimen, I'll have you know," cried Miss Hester from behind me. "How dreadful of you to talk that way."

Now Dr. Blessed looked at Miss Hester, then down at us. He spoke slowly to her. "It is not dreadful at all. It's my life's work. I don't think we are understanding one another properly. This gentleman, I believe, has matters confused. I think I understand now, though. I believe he thinks I have come here to see a human being. That is not the case." He turned to Dr. Alf. "I am not a medical doctor, but a cetologist attached to the University of Chicago. I have come about the whale." He nodded his head and asked, "I presume there *is* a dead whale here?"

"A cetologist? Well, well," grunted Dr. Alf, who I could tell didn't know what a "cetologist" was either.

"Yes, I study whales. I've chased whales over much of the earth. I want your whale."

"Why?" asked Sarah.

He went on speaking to Dr. Alf. "I want its skeleton to take back with me. It will become part of a museum exhibit in Chicago." Now he turned back to Miss Hester to say, "I see nothing dreadful in this, do you, miss?"

I looked behind me and saw how she had turned pink. Blushing became her dark good looks.

Now Dr. Blessed turned back to Dr. Perkins to say, "I had just arrived in San Francisco after examining a rare whale in Japan when I read about your humpback here. I sent a telegram to my museum and they wired me to get up here fast, so I wired you. Dr. Perkins, you were quoted in the newspaper piece as one of the people in charge of the whale problem."

"I'm not exactly in charge, but I'm mighty interested. Can you help us with the carcass?"

Dr. Blessed went on. "Yes, I intend to boil it down."

"*Boil* it?" exploded Sarah.

"Yes, whale blubber is fat and boils down to make oil."

Evangeline asked suspiciously, "Where are you going to boil our whale?"

"On the beach, where I suspect you've left it—given its size."

Dr. Alf chuckled. "Given its size, that's where it is."

"Who'll boil it?" asked Miss Hester.

"Local men, I trust. My museum will pay them to cut off the blubber and boil it." Now he spoke to Dr. Alf. "Who is this problem person at the hotel? She had something to do with the beach, too, I presume."

"That's true. She's an unfortunate young woman who came ashore from a shipwreck last winter tied to a mast. We don't know who she is or where she's from, though we've left no stone unturned to find out." Dr. Alf took off his derby and scratched the top of his head. "The Peninsula men will be most happy to work for you and get paid for getting rid of the whale before tourist season and the hot weather comes. Put your baggage in my rig and I'll take you to the hotel. By the way, I don't know if the whale is a male or a female."

As Dr. Blessed picked up his bags and put them into the buggy, he asked, "How long is it?"

"Around forty-five feet."

"Then it's probably a male. Humpback males run smaller than the females. If it'd been fifty feet or over, I'd have said . . ." His voice trailed off as he got into the rig, and Dr. Alf clucked to Rosinante to get moving.

Once the people doctor and the whale doctor were

on their way, I said, "Oh, my golly, they'll be boiling down a whale right here where we can watch it!"

I saw Miss Hester clutch her portfolio to her bosom. She said, "Oh, yes. Tomorrow we'll study more about whales, and we'll do some of it at the beach, perhaps. Oh, how timely this is. Why, Dr. Blessed is a real blessed miracle, isn't he?"

Sarah touched me with her elbow and said loudly, "He's the handsomest man who's come to Nahcotta in a long time. I wonder if he's single?" She winked at me, then bent to whisper into Evangeline's ear, pushing aside some yellow curls to do it.

A fast runner, Evangeline was off in a flash, sprinting for the buggy. She ran beside it for a while, then ran back to us shouting, "He isn't married. I just asked him. I told him our teacher wanted to know."

Miss Hester cried out, "Evangeline! How could you do such a wicked thing? I never asked you to do that!"

"It was easy, Hester. I can run faster than old Rosinante can trot. Dr. Blessed said he was kept too busy tracking whales to find himself a wife, but he says he isn't against the idea. I think you better work fast, though. He says boiling down a whale won't take too long with a lot of men working, and he hopes to leave with the skeleton in a week."

I thought Miss Hester might faint, her face got so red. How embarrassed she must be by her sisters. To protect them, I told her, "Please don't be mad.

Evangeline doesn't understand things like love at first sight and courting yet. She's too young for that. In books I read that comes later on in life to ladies." Then, to change the subject, I added, "Say, I wonder what the men will boil the whale fat in."

Evangeline said, "Dr. Blessed told me that, too. He says big crab pots with fires lit under them will do the job just fine. It isn't exactly the first whale he's ever boiled."

Miss Hester said weakly, "Ma's going to hear about what you did, Evangeline. She won't let it go by without giving you a good talking-to. So you got yet another question in, too? Did you happen to find out Dr. Blessed's middle name and his favorite color?"

"No, I didn't have time for that."

Miss Hester was angry. "I'm not sure now that I'll take the school to the beach tomorrow after all."

"Oh, please," said Sarah.

"Pretty please," begged Evangeline, guilty as she was.

"With sugar on it," said I.

"With sugar and cream," said Florence.

Alec didn't say anything, probably because he couldn't think of any more goodies to add.

Miss Hester let out a sigh. "All right, we'll go, children. It will be educational for you. But we mustn't ever get in the way."

By the time we all got to the beach the next morning, a little after eight, Mama and Mr. and Mrs. Kimball and everybody else on the Peninsula were there. The word that "blubber boilers" were wanted had spread fast. Lots of men had brought their big black crab pots along with them in the backs of their wagons.

We all watched Dr. Blessed show them how to slice blubber. They were to make long cuts with long knives and roll the fat away, cut it up, and put it into the pots, then pour the fat out onto the sand once it was liquid. It was messy, but it was the only thing they could do with the fat, and it seeped quickly into the sand.

The whale smelled really bad now, but we could still breathe the air without holding handkerchiefs over our faces. All of us school kids sat at a distance from the blubber boilers on the sand dunes.

Miss Hester told us, "What they are doing is called 'flensing' a whale. Fifty years ago people used whale oil in their lamps. Now we use kerosene, which is a coal product. There's no truly important use for whale oil anymore. Some people eat whale meat, but in this country few do. I'm glad we don't. They are such wonderful animals. Well, it seems we are to have a visitor."

Dr. Blessed came striding up to where we sat in the dunes and asked Miss Hester, "Would you care to stroll around the whale with me, you and your children? I can tell you some things about it and other whales if you would like me to."

Sarah said, "Oh, we'd love that. Can we go, Hester?"

"*May* we go, Sarah. Yes, that would be very nice."

And so we all got up and walked onto the hard sand and strolled around the whale, listening to Dr. Blessed.

He said, "This is a very old whale, perhaps over thirty years old. I'd say it died of old age more than anything else. You can see it has been harpooned once, and the wound has healed over." He pointed to a gash in its side as long as I was tall. Then he went on to talk about fins and tails and blowholes and how there were whales in all the oceans of the world. Some were rare. Some were common, like cachalots, or sperm whales. Some were not gray at all, but black and white, like killer whales, or pure white, like beluga whales from Arctic waters. Some were very big, like the blue whale. Others were quite small—for whales, that is. Some made singing noises, like the humpback here. Others were silent.

When he finished, we asked questions, and then Miss Hester thanked him and told us we'd better go back to school and let him get on with his work.

As we turned to leave, he told her, "I have a name other than Dr. Blessed, Miss Kimball. It's Peter. May I call you Hester? I gather that is your name."

I watched her closely. So did her sisters and Florence. Yes, she smiled at him. Then she said, "It is Hester, Peter," and she led us away.

Sarah nudged me. "I'd say he's a fast worker, wouldn't you, Marcy?"

As we got up to the dunes we'd been sitting on, we saw the Palace Hotel wagon coming along the plank road toward us.

Evangeline yelled, "Hey, that's Aunt Rose and Uncle Ced. Look who they've got with them! It's the lady from the ocean."

Yes, it was Mr. Perkins driving the hotel wagon. Beside him on the seat sat his wife and the lady from the sea.

When they were next to us, he reined in and said, "We fetched our star boarder down here to see the whale before it disappears."

I looked at her. Her golden eyes were fixed on the whale, not on us. Of course I knew why. She saw us often—most likely she never got to see a whale.

Mrs. Perkins told us, "You'd best say good-bye to Anna here. She and I will be leaving Sunday for Fort Steilacoom where the asylum is. Come, children, shake her hand."

One by one we came forward, reached up, took the lady's cool, limp hand, and shook it. But she didn't even seem to see us. She was looking only at the whale.

Now she stood up in the wagon, pointed straight at the whale, and said one loud word, "Keet!" She paused for a few seconds and added, "Kashalot neyet belooka," and shook her head.

Katchalot—belooga? Those words stuck in my memory. Where had I heard them? Suddenly I knew. Dr. Blessed had just used them talking about whales.

One was a sperm and the other was an Arctic white whale.

The Arctic? But this lady wasn't any Eskimo, for sure.

I didn't wait a second to ask Miss Hester's permission to go. I tore away from the others and ran down to where Dr. Blessed was standing beside a blubber pot as the hissing oil was dumped.

I caught hold of his coat and gasped out, just as Sarah pounded up behind me, "Dr. Blessed, there's somebody in a wagon up in the dunes we want you to try to talk to. She just said some words you used— 'katchalot' and 'belooga'."

" 'Belooga'? 'Katchalot'?" He looked surprised and puzzled.

"Yes, sir. She pointed to your whale and that's what she said."

Sarah tugged at my arm. "No, Marcy, you didn't hear her right. I was closer to her than you were. She said 'belooka' and 'kashalot.' There was a real clear *k* and *sh* in what I heard her say."

The whale expert looked amazed. "Why, those are the Russian names for two types of whales. 'Kashalot' is their word for a sperm whale, and the 'belooka' is a small white one."

Russian?

I cried out, "Come with us to talk to the lady from the sea, the one Dr. Alf told you about. Maybe you're the one who can talk to her."

He nodded. "Well, I shall try. I know a bit of Russian from my travels."

Up we went to the wagon where the washed-up lady sat, her eyes still on the whale.

Dr. Blessed walked to her side, took off his derby, bowed, and said, "Zdrasti barishna zoevoot Petter Blessed. Oo menya keet." He pointed to the whale. "Neyet kashalot—neyet belooka."

She exploded with a whole string of excited words. "Da, da, keet, bolshoy keet! Harrashow!"

She *understood* and was answering him. She could talk! She went on talking and talking while tears rolled down her face, and he kept saying over and over, "Pajalsta, medlenno, medlenno," until she stopped.

# 12
## ANNA FROM THE SEA

Dr. Blessed turned to the Perkinses and said, "I badly needed to sleep after my long trip here if I was to get up early this morning and start my work. If I had met her last night, I could have solved your problem earlier, perhaps. I'm sorry I didn't. She's a Siberian Russian from the Aleutian Islands off the east coast of Siberia. I've been there several times. 'Keet,' 'belooka,' and 'kashalot' refer to different types of whales in her language, as you probably have guessed. She's seen whales of several kinds because there's a lot of whaling done in those waters. She thought this was a sperm whale, what we call a cachalot, you see?"

Everybody was silent with shock for a moment. "So that's it?" Ced Perkins finally said with a long whistle. "Rose, you hang onto the reins while I run and tell Alf the good news. He's wandering around that whale like he would some hospital ward."

Miss Hester asked, "So that's what she is—Siberian?"

I wanted to know, "What happened to her? Ask her that, please, Dr. Blessed."

He spoke to her again in the language that seemed to me full of *p*s and *k*s, and she answered. As she did, she put her hands to her face and cried some more.

At last he said softly to all of us, "Her mother was on that ship that foundered in a storm. Her mother's eyes were bad. This girl was on her way with her to see an eye specialist in San Francisco when the storm hit. The ship was on the point of sinking, so the sailors lashed the girl to the mast and threw it overboard into the ocean. She says her father lives in the Aleutians, and she wants to go home. She grieves for her mother."

Sarah asked, "What's 'mother' in Russian?"

" 'Mott'."

I took a guess and said, "How do you say 'father' in Russian?"

" 'Ah-teeyets'."

"My word," breathed Miss Hester. "You do know a great deal, don't you, Peter?"

"Oh, not so much, Hester."

Just then Dr. Alf came running up. He acted delighted. He said, "So she's a Siberian Russian and she speaks well? I imagine she was just hurt and scared and lonesome here among strangers and foreigners."

I looked at her and saw she'd stopped crying. That was good.

Mrs. Perkins asked, "What will we do with her now, Alf?"

"I've been thinking on that, Rose. San Francisco is a big city. I suspect there's a Russian consul there. Siberia and the Aleutians are part of Russia. I'll find out if there is a consul there. If there is, I'll telegraph him to get somebody up here to get her. The consul can see to it that she gets back home. That's what consuls do."

I asked, "Why didn't she know her own country when she saw Russia on the map of the world? It's too big to be missed."

"Marcella, it's my educated guess that she's never been in Russia. It's a long, long way from the Aleutian Islands—thousands of miles—and I believe there's no railroad across Siberia yet. I'll bet she was born in the Aleutians and has been there all her life until now. That explains why she'd never seen a train."

Mrs. Perkins asked Dr. Blessed, "Will you please ask her if she can read and write?"

He spoke some more Russian words and then shook his head. "She says 'neyet.' That means 'no'."

Dr. Alf nodded. "That's another reason why she couldn't read her name in the Bible."

Mrs. Perkins laughed as she put her arm around the lady from the sea. "Tonight she can talk in Russian to her heart's content with Dr. Blessed here."

The whale hunter gave her a smile. "Whoa, my Russian's not that good! I'll try for her sake, though."

As we kids started off with our teacher, I heard Sarah speak to her aunt. Because I was standing close to them, I could hear her say softly, "Aunt Rose, Hester calls Dr. Blessed 'Peter' already. I bet she snags him. I never saw her take to anybody so fast before."

"Not any Peninsula man," agreed Dr. Alf, who'd eavesdropped on Sarah's words. "Hester's sort of particular. She's been badly hurt by Whitney's death, too. They fought like cats and dogs, but underneath they were very close, being the two oldest. Maybe this young man's coming here will snap her out of her sadness." He chuckled. "Odd, isn't it? Our two big troubles get taken care of in two days—*bang, bang!*"

"And all thanks to a young man who chases whales and travels a lot," said Sarah's aunt.

I mused out loud, "Gosh, all three of them came out of nowhere, didn't they? The lady from the sea, the whale, and Dr. Blessed—like they'd been sent to us."

"Three's enough in the way of sendings," said Ced Perkins.

"It's surely made for an interesting year," came from Mrs. Perkins, "but it's been too interesting for me some of the time. Sweet as this Siberian girl is, she has been a chore."

Sarah had the final word. It was to me. "Marcy, just think what you would have missed if you'd gone back home to Portland last September. Aren't you glad you didn't go?"

I turned to Mama, who by now was beside me. She'd heard the question, and said softly, "I think I'm glad we didn't—even if I do miss my husband badly."

I told Sarah, "If we had gone, we'd never have got to know you Kimballs, and we've liked that."

Florence added, "That's a true fact, Sarah."

"It sure is," agreed Alec.


Getting rid of our whale went fast with so many men cutting it up and boiling it down. That was good, because it was messy work, and it smelled more and more every day.

When the men got down to the skeleton, they cut it apart with Dr. Blessed giving orders. They wrapped the pieces in tarpaulins that he numbered and recorded in a little notebook, then carried the bundles to the train depot in wagons.

Dr. Blessed and the skeleton were due to leave on Monday morning.

Saturday night there was a band concert in Nahcotta. All of us Abbotts went. We saw Dr. Blessed there with Miss Hester in the third row. She had on a pretty peach-colored taffeta dress and wore honeysuckle blossoms in her dark hair. They looked like stars.

When I asked Sarah the next morning how things had gone between the doctor and her big sister, she told me, "Hester didn't come home till two in the morning."

I asked, "What happened? The concert was over at nine o'clock."

"I don't know. But she and Dr. Blessed sat out on our front porch in the moonlight until four o'clock."

Florence asked hopefully, "Did he kiss and hug her?"

"I don't know," Sarah sighed. "Evangeline and I climbed out my bedroom window and flopped down on the roof over the front porch to listen in on them, but we couldn't see them."

I asked, "Did you at least hear what they were saying?"

"Marcy, that was disappointing, too. They talked too low for us to hear much, but we did hear him promise he'd write to her."

I said, "Hugs and kisses don't make any noise."

Evangeline shrugged her shoulders. "He sounded to me like he looked forward to hunting some more whales. He did invite her to Chicago to see the skeleton when he's got it all wired up together and on display. But he said that will take a while."

I said, "That doesn't sound romantic to me."

"But it might be to him," said Sarah. "Remember, he did ask her to Chicago, didn't he? He wants to see her again." She nudged me. "Hester's a dandy letter writer. She'll keep him on the string that way if she wants to."

We didn't see Dr. Blessed and the whale bones leave Nahcotta because of school, but we saw the man who was sent by the Russian consul in San Francisco. He came in on the train the Saturday after Dr. Blessed and the whale skeleton left. The Russian was dark while the lady was pale. He was tall and elegant in a long black frock coat and top hat. His sharp-pointed beard was black, too.

We knew when he'd be arriving because the consul telegraphed Dr. Alf the time, so we were all at the depot to see him come. After he'd shaken hands with Dr. Alf and Ced Perkins, he did something that made the Kimball girls gasp. He kissed the hands of Mrs. Kimball, Miss Hester, Mrs. Perkins, and Mama.

He said in a deep, accented voice, "It is my desire to take Miss Anna Ivanovna Sokolov back to San Francisco with me as soon as possible and send her home to her father."

Dr. Alf told him, "You can take her on the train

that leaves at four this afternoon. That's what she needs—to go home. Come to the hotel now. She's waiting for you." He pointed to us. "These are the children who found her on the beach." And he introduced Sarah and me and Evangeline and Alec and Florence.

The Russian bowed to each of us. Alec bowed, while Florence and I curtseyed as we'd been taught, and the Kimball sisters copied us. He smiled at our fine manners and said to us, "The government of the Tsar of all the Russias thanks you for the care you have given to one of our citizens and wishes me to thank you. Spasiba."

Spasiba—another Russian word. It had to mean "thank you".

He turned back to the Perkinses and Dr. Alf. "I have brought money with me to repay you for her keep and for your medical services."

"My wife and I don't want any money," said Ced Perkins.

"I don't, either," came from Dr. Alf.

"But the Tsar would want you to have it."

Mr. Perkins told him, "No, sir, just you tell him we Americans like to be hospitable when we can."

Again the Russian bowed. He put the velvet purse back into his coat pocket and said, "Do not be surprised, then, if the Tsar sends all of you medals."

Ced Perkins looked shocked, then laughed. "That'd

be something to put on the hotel wall for guests to see."

Alec asked what I wanted to know but was too polite to ask. "What kind of medals? How big will they be?"

"The kind that you hang around your neck with a ribbon, my boy."

"My word!" exclaimed Mama.

Mrs. Perkins invited us all to go up to the hotel to say farewell to the lady from the sea. After we had cake and coffee and tea in the hotel parlor, we went up to the lady and said, "Good-bye," and each and every one of us kissed her. We girls each gave her a clove-studded apple pomander ball to remember us by every time she smelled it. Anna Ivanovna Sokolov kissed us back, and we saw her smile for the first time. She had dimples in each cheek. How pretty she was— not like a snow princess anymore but like a real, live lady.

We saw her and the Russian man off at the depot, of course.

How lovely our lady from the sea looked as she stood at the end of the very last railroad car, number three, with the Russian. She held tight to the bouquet of wildflowers we'd picked for her and waved and waved until we couldn't see her anymore.

We heard her cry out to us in Russian as she waved, "Spasiba. Dosveedonya." That last word had to be Russian for "farewell".

Summer came, with Sarah and me and Florence and Alec and other Peninsula kids picking wild strawberries, digging clams, and raking crabs. Sarah and I graduated from the eighth grade, too. Now we had something else to think about—high school. High school among a lot of real big kids. We'd find that hard after being the oldest at Miss Hester's school. We'd have to ride on the train twenty miles back and forth to Ilwaco five days a week. Sarah's papa had saved money for years to pay her tuition. Papa had written us he could find enough money to pay mine. Sarah and I would be together!

Papa came to Ocean Park for July Fourth, looking better than he had when we'd seen him at Easter. He came with us while we took Prince Albert strolling on the hot beach under his umbrella. Papa said we were "chestnut brown" and, oh, how we'd grown this year!

For dinner, Mama served creamed chicken with our garden peas in patty shells and biscuits, with cream puffs for dessert.

We had plenty of cream from the neighbor's cows and had bought rock salt at the Nahcotta store. We'd decided that we'd make ice cream for a nighttime treat the night of the Fourth.

While Mama and Papa sat side by side in the porch glider, Florence, Alec, and I sat on the front steps taking turns with the handle of the ice cream freezer. While we cranked, we told Papa about the lady from the sea and the whale and the whale hunter and the Russian from San Francisco, though we had written him all this before.

At the end of our story, he said, "You've had some year, haven't you? You didn't miss Portland much, huh?"

"Not one bit," said Alec.

"We like it here," came from Florence.

"We made good friends, Papa," I told him.

"Well, remember when I was here at Easter I told you I was working on a surprise? Here it is! We'll be leaving here come September and won't be back until next June."

I stopped cranking. "For Portland again?"

"No. For Astoria. I've sold all our Portland property, got a loan, and bought a new store over the Columbia River. It's another dry goods store, mostly fabrics, and not so large and fancy as the one in Portland. But I like the location—it's on a corner. I've already got my eye on a house to rent in Astoria. I inspected it before I came up here this time."

I asked, "Will I go to high school there?"

"Yes, we'll find money for you to go."

I let out a sigh. Sorrow grabbed me as I thought of Sarah, who'd be going to school in Ilwaco over the Columbia River from me. She'd been the best friend I'd ever had. I told Papa, "The Kimballs have been really kind and good to us. My friend Sarah's some-body I hate to leave."

Florence added, "I don't want to leave Evangeline."

He told us, "I can understand your not wanting to leave. I had school friends I liked, too."

I couldn't see Papa in the dark, but I could tell by the tone of his voice that he was thinking. After a bit he said, "I can't open a store here. There wouldn't be enough customers to make it pay. Those Peninsula girls could come visit you in Astoria whenever they want to, and you can come visit here on weekends. The Astoria house is big enough for guests. You can come here to live in the summers if you want to, or we can rent this house to summer people. I don't plan to sell it. But don't worry, Marcella, you ought to see a good deal of your friend."

Oh, Sarah. It would still be *Sarah and me!* I knew my grammar was bad, but how good those words sounded. All year here it'd been "Sarah and me and the lady from the sea" in my head because it rhymed. I'd tell Sarah first thing in the morning about our going over the Columbia to live. She had liked Astoria, the biggest place she'd ever seen. So had I. It wasn't as big as Portland by a long shot, but it had more restaurants than Nahcotta or Ilwaco, and a theater and stores to shop around in with lots of interesting things in them. It'd be fun to visit all these places with Sarah and show her my "city ways," though I liked Peninsula ways better now.

I had grabbed hold of the freezer crank hard and ran it round and round when Mama started to talk. She was saying, "Henry, I don't think I'll need household help in Astoria—maids and a cook, I mean. I am perfectly capable by now of caring for my family and a house with the help of the children. Look what they can do now. I never cared for teas and socials and visiting down in Portland, and I've lost my longing for fancy gowns. You've enjoyed my cooking. After all, you sent me a Christmas cookbook of French cuisine. I cooked what I could with the ingredients I was able to find here, though there are no truffles to be located anywhere. I'll never be afraid of a stove again. I believe I have a born talent for cooking. I wish to speak with you about our dessert tonight. Did you like your cream puff?"

"It was capital, A-one, light as air and crunchy at the same time. No chef in Portland could do better than you did, and those strawberry preserves of yours were delicious."

"Thank you, Henry dear. I've inquired around and learned that there are no fancy bakeries in Astoria. I wish to speak with you about puff pastry. What would you think if I started a modest little pastry shop in Astoria?"

"Lord in heaven, Nelline, you *want* to go to *work?*"

Papa might have been surprised at what she'd just said, but the three of us weren't. We knew Mama better by now. In time she'd get her way with him. In her mind, Mama had already named her Astoria shop "Patisserie Abbott." She'd told me that.

Florence whispered to me, "Do you think he'll give in to her? He isn't used to ladies running businesses."

I whispered back, "They'll argue about it, but she'll wear him down. Mama's stronger than she used to be—a lot stronger now."

"She will," was all Alec said as he took the crank from my freezing hand.

Mama went on, "Henry, it's what I really want—to have my own little business. You will have yours and I will have mine. It won't cost us much for me to start. It will only be a very small enterprise—that is, to start with. . . ."

I listened to my mother and smiled in the dark.

# AUTHOR'S NOTE

Over a span of twenty years, many librarians and children have asked me to write a sequel to my 1964 book, *The Nickel-Plated Beauty.* (In 1972 I wrote a companion piece to it called *O, The Red Rose Tree,* but it was not a sequel. Only Dr. Alf Perkins and his horse, Rosinante, are common to these two books.)

*The Nickel-Plated Beauty* was set in 1886. *Sarah and Me and the Lady from the Sea,* which is not truly a sequel but also a companion piece, opens nine years later, in 1895, with a non-Kimball narrator from Oregon and with only three of the Kimballs' large family of children from the first book as main characters—Sarah, Hester (the narrator of *The Nickel-Plated Beauty*), and Evangeline, who is born at the end of the first book. Other Kimballs are at the edges of this story with their parents and Peninsula relatives, the Perkinses of the Palace Hotel. The narrator of *Sarah and Me and the Lady from the Sea* is a well-to-do and better-educated Portlander.

Young readers and some older ones will think perhaps that I exaggerate the helplessness of the society women of the 1890s. I do not. Surrounded by servants all their lives, they knew nothing of housework except to give orders. Fathers and husbands protected them from any kind of work and any knowledge of the harshness of the lives of working women of that era. Some rich families arranged marriages for their daughters and saw to it that they met only "their social equals."

Surely readers will want to know about the shipwrecked lady. Was she real? She is fictional. However, shipwrecks were common along the Peninsula beaches at the Columbia River's mouth. It was customary for Peninsula people to take in and nurse castaways. Once an entire crew of Frenchmen, unable to speak any English, was shipwrecked there. Imagine the consternation among the people of the small towns who spoke only English! My inspiration for the lady from the Aleutian Islands came from this incident. Ships from Alaska and other ports of call constantly plied Washington coast waters. Not all would have carried telegraphic equipment in 1895 to wire for help. Ships can and do go down at sea and leave no wreckage to float ashore. Someone tied to a mast is a romantic concept, but it has happened in real life when no other course to save the person was available.

Dead whales wash ashore all over the world. They present a definite disposal problem—the bigger the whale, the larger the problem. Much more is known today about the deep-diving humpback whale than was known in the 1890s. It does "sing" to communicate with its fellows. Its ear has a special construction that intrigues modern scientists, who want to learn why it can dive so deep. It is being studied right now.

Some people are going to scoff at my way of solving the trouble with my whale. I suggest they had better not! There is a factual precedent for this also. In the first ten years of the twentieth century, a dead humpback whale did come ashore on the ocean side of the Washington Peninsula. The news of its presence spread swiftly by telegraph. A scientist read of it and came posthaste to the beaches in search of the skeleton. He hired Peninsula men to cut up the whale and boil down its blubber to reach the skeleton. Then he took the bones back east with him to a museum, where they were reassembled and displayed.

I have described the Peninsula and the Astoria of the 1890s as old photographs show them. People from

Finland made up a goodly share of Astoria's population, so my Astoria doctor could certainly be a Finn.

High schools charged tuition in the 1890s; grammar schools were free. As a result, many people of that time never had more than an eighth-grade education.

The 1894 flood in Portland, Oregon, is history. A number of businesses were bankrupted by it. Portlanders who maintained summer places on the Peninsula were forced to sell them.

The Kimballs are modeled somewhat on my mother's Ocean Park pioneer family. My mother is the last one living. All of her brothers and sisters are gone by now. My mother's aunt operated a hotel and eating house in Nahcotta. Her husband was the brother of the town doctor, but his name was not Perkins. I have a very old snapshot of this doctor standing with my grandfather, both bearded and very serious, in front of the picket fence of my grandfather's house. The date on the back says 1909. Photograph paper endures longer than people do. I know the little doctor was loved by many, so I imagine he must have been a Dr. Alf of sorts to have attracted so much affection.

Perhaps some readers will be interested in the Russian words I've used. They are not in the Russian script, which could scarcely be pronounced in English unless the Russian alphabet is known. I have sounded these words out phonetically to approximate Russian pronunciations English-speaking children can read.

Some words I identified as they were used in the story. Others I have not but will do so here. "Zdrasti" translates into "greetings". "Barishna" means "Miss". "Neyet" is "no" or "not". "Zoevoot" comes out to be "I am named," "Oo menya keet" to "I have a whale here," "bolshoy keet" to "a big whale," "harrashow" to "good," "pajalsta" to a shortened form of "please," and "medlenno" to "slow".

Though I have studied Russian for more than ten years myself with my professor husband, I have asked the advice of Dr. Louis A. Pedrotti and Dr. Selim Karady of the Russian Department of the University of California, Riverside, for the simplest English child-usable pronunciations closest to the actual Russian. Accustomed to teaching college students, they found this an entertaining challenge.

I must thank my mother, Jessie P. Robbins, for her help on several points, and librarian Sherry Rosselius of the Seattle King County Library System for some needed geographical data. I also say "thank you" to librarians Peter Bliss (the "physical model" for my Dr. Blessed, with Dr. Bliss's amused permission) and Lorelei Tanji of the University of California, Riverside, library.

*Patricia Beatty*
MAY 1988